M000105371

Love,
Revolution,
&
Lemonade

Love,
Revolution,
&
Lemonade

HANNAH L. DRAKE

Drake Publishing

Love, Revolution, & Lemonade
Copyright ©2019 by Hannah L. Drake
Published by Drake Publishing ISBN-13: 9780997299212

Printed in the United States of America.

All rights reserved. No part of this book may be reproduced, stored in, or introduced into a retrieval system or transmitted, in any form or by any means (electronic, mechanical, photocopying, recording, or otherwise), without the expressed written consent of the author.

Author Photo: Jessie Kriech-Higdon www.kriech-higdonphoto.com

Cover Art : Christa Harris Facebook:Positively Peculiar LLC

DEDICATION

Perhaps the tenth time is a charm. After years of writing, and giving all my words to the world, this tenth book is dedicated to me; the broken girl that picked up the pieces to become the woman I am today. A woman that has Loved and when I Love, I Love and I Love hard. A woman that has stood on the front lines of Revolution, that fights for Revolution, that longs for true Revolution. And a woman that has found a way to make Lemonade out of a life of lemons.

There are so many facets to being a woman. For too many years I allowed others to dictate what being a woman means for me. I was too concerned about being judged, being criticized, fearful of being a woman that enjoys having an amazingly wet orgasm. Fearful of being a woman that chooses to love whoever she wants to love. Until I decided I was no longer afraid. At some point you have to make a decision to live. And even when fear starts to rear its head, I've decided to just write it how I feel it and let the chips fall where they may.

I started of writing Love, Revolution, & Lemonade too many times to count. I thought of it during the height of my poem, Formation going viral. I couldn't understand why I was so hesitant to write this book. Every time I started it, something came up and I would put it on the backburner. I realized that sometimes we are not yet ready to write the things that we want to write, need to write, and should write. Now when I look back on it, I know that I was not prepared. I still had a lot of life to live, I still had some past hurts to deal with to pour into this book and some truths to face about myself. Everything is always in its proper season. For everyone that asked me, "Hannah, when is the next collection of poetry coming out," thank you for being patient and allowing me the time to go through this part of my journey. While this book is dedicated to me, I hope that you find something in the pages that resonates with you. I hope you continue on your own journey and become the person that you are destined to be.

CONTENTS

Dedication iv
To My Readers vii
Love **8-59**
The Fabric Of Our Lives 12
The Greatest Man I Never Knew 14
The Best Part of Me is Laying On A Mattress 25
Teuscher Chocolate 27
An Idea 30
Unashamed 32
Fuck **34**
Dance for Me 35
I Taught Him That 45
I Taught Her That 46
Lick Me 47
Love, Sex, And Revolution 48
Seasons of Joy 51
Contours & Curves 53
Could This Be? 56
She Smells Like 58
Unafraid 59
Revolution **60-108**
Formation 62
Spaces 63
We Are Not Ragdolls 65
Strange Fruit 67
Something About The Rain 68
Ain't I A Mother? 69
You Were Born to Be A Problem 72
Everybody Wants To Be Black Until It's Time to Be Black 75
All You Had To Do Was Play the Game, Boy 76
Master's Shadow 78
Who Protects Black Women? 79

By Any Means Necessary   82
Teardrops & Trust Funds   84
Why Are You Angry, White Man?   86
Do Not Move Off the Sidewalk Challenge: Holding   87
Your Space In A White World
Working 9-5 In White Spaces   93
Nana   98
Change Dwells In The Realm of the Uncomfortable   101
Compassion Rising   104
Sacred Wisdom of Love   107
Lemonade   **109-136**

Lemonade   110
My Life Lemonade   111
Finding Me   112
Power   114
I, Too, Am Serena. Tales of Being A Black Woman   117
With A Voice
Black Swans Swimming Upstream   125
For Colored Girls Who Considered Suicide When   126
Lemonade is Enuf
Break Yourself   128
Dawn   131
I Am Becoming   133
Love, Revolution, and Lemonade   136

To My Readers

For those that started out with me during my first collection of poetry, Hannah's Plea-Poetry for the Soul and for those new readers that are just now discovering who I am, welcome. I am so thankful that you have chosen Love, Revolution & Lemonade.

I had one assignment with this book, to tell the truth. And anyone that has ever dealt with the truth, you know it can be messy. Truth often, if not always, means exposure and who likes being exposed? But if I am going to be true to who I am, who I am becoming, I have to tell the truth. My life hasn't always been and still ain't rainbows and sunshine. This book will probably be one of my REALEST books but I wouldn't do it if I didn't believe that my truth will set someone free even if that someone is just me. This ain't reserved Hannah. This is Hannah, who Hannah is – real, raw, honest, uncut. So if you ain't feeling that, now is the time to stop reading. This is not the book for you. But if you are open on going through a journey of Love, Revolution & Lemonade, please continue through the pages.

Thank you, for always supporting me and thank you, for even challenging me.

Everything that I know has led me to this moment of Love, Revolution, & Lemonade.

LOVE

LOVE

noun

\ ˈləv \

Definition of *love*

1a(1): strong affection for another arising out of kinship or personal ties maternal *love* for a child

(2): attraction based on sexual desire : affection and tenderness felt by lovers After all these years, they are still very much in *love.*

(3): affection based on admiration, benevolence, or common interests *love* for his old schoolmates

When I think about my past relationships, it wasn't until I was older that it dawned on me that I had to go all the way back to the beginning.

I try to think about how I first learned how to love?

I don't think anyone ever taught me how to love or reflected love in front of me.

My mother and father always seem to be on a collision course and we were the collateral damage.

LOVE

1a(1)): strong affection for another arising out of kinship or personal ties maternal *love* for a child

THE FABRIC OF OUR LIVES

I wish that she loved me
The way that I needed her to love me
It wasn't until I was 40 that I understood
That she could not love me that way

Because she didn't know how to love me

No one ever loved her the way a mother should love a daughter
She was never taught how to love herself; so how could she love me?

I was asking her for something that was foreign to her
I needed something from her that she was incapable of giving

We were like two people, facing each other screaming in two different
languages
Both shouting to be heard
Longing to be understood
Oblivious to the fact that our shouts were falling on deaf ears
Not because we didn't want to understand each other
We just couldn't

We didn't talk about the past
Our relationship was a quilt of mismatched secrets
But one day in a moment of vulnerability
She told me a story of her being a little girl
Standing in a cotton field picking cotton
For eighty cents a day

It was the first time that I saw my mother
Really... saw... my... mother

Not as the woman but as the little girl
Skin blackened from the sun
Legs covered in red dust
Little hands that pulled cotton from boils
Skin that was pricked and bled from the sharp casings that covered the cotton
boils
Cotton that would never be spun into beautiful dresses for girls that didn't
look like her

The fabric of her life would be sewn together by pain and dysfunction
Her grandmother would come pick her up each day to go to the cotton fields
She worked to make money so her family could buy bologna and bread for
dry sandwiches as sustenance

I asked her does she remember anyone before her grandmother
She doesn't

Her stories have intentional gaps
Things she doesn't want to remember or repeat
It finally dawned on me that even she has stories she keeps hidden…like me

I was finally at age where I could see her
Where I could free her from the prison of expectations
People can only give you what they have to give
She was at a place that didn't allow for me to disrupt her peace
There was comfort in the demons that she knew
They understood each other
As long as no one came along to upset their flow she could deal with tolerate
them

I allowed her space

I love her the way she allows me to love her
From afar because I understand now
Loving her up close is just too painful

THE GREATEST MAN I NEVER KNEW

"Come home."

It was two words I never thought I would hear from my Dad. I hadn't seen my father in years, and now I stood in the community room of a battered woman's shelter, payphone to my ear hearing the voice of a man that I had long forgotten tell me and my three-year-old daughter to come home.

I would like to say I don't know how I ended up in that shelter but I do, bad decisions followed by wrong choices led me there. My mother had kicked me out of the house when I was just 16. I ended up staying with a boyfriend and his family until I graduated. I managed to graduate in the top ten percent of my high school class. Every college I applied to, I was accepted. I sent my mother a graduation invitation. She never replied. I don't know if she was at my high school graduation or not. She says she was there. I never saw her, and so began my journey in life. But the course of my life had been set years before I walked across that stage and received my high school diploma. My childhood was a childhood of hell peppered with moments of heaven. Dinnertime was always together. I played Barbie's with my friend Meagan who lived across the street. I read books, lots of books. My dad was an avid reader. I read the encyclopedia and National Geographic. I read Encyclopedia Brown, Ramona Quimby and Are You There God? It's Me, Margaret. I always asked God, "Are you there? It's me, Hannah." God never seemed to answer me. Never seemed to care about the horror going on in my house.

I do not recall what I did. I wish I could. I have searched my mind a million times to remember. I suppose that memory is buried deep in a place that I do not want to go. Whatever I did I know I was getting in big trouble. Spankings were not just spankings in my house. They were events. Events that caused shadows and whispers to descend on the house, shut up the curtains, lock the doors and keep love from coming in. The hits were swifts as I laid across the stairs to take my beating. There is no other way to describe it- it was a beating. Not with a switch but a 2×4, connecting with my nine-year-old flesh. I remember crying and my body turning just as the piece of wood came down and landed against my left knee. My body buckled spilling underneath me like ice on hot concrete. I laid there as my body transformed into a puddle. No one comforted me. Tears were for fools in this house. I remember my mom wrapped an ace bandage around my knee as if that would make my now sideways facing knee socket go back into place. It didn't. The pain was excruciating. I limped to the bathroom, to the kitchen to my bedroom. To this day I believe my father felt proud of what he did in that moment. He had shown me he was bigger, stronger, more powerful than I would ever be.

I went to school the next day. My teacher asked me about my knee. I lied. We always knew to lie. "What happens in this house stays in this house." I was conditioned to keep the secrets. Always keep the secrets.

I swallowed secrets down like sour candy. My tongue adjusting to the shock of the bitterness before accepting it as normal. This is how families are, right? No one took me to the doctor. My father wrote my prescription, yelled it out to me as if my weirdly placed kneecap was bothering him. Perhaps he felt guilty every time he saw me limping around. "Ride your bike!" That is it. That was the prescription. Every day I came home from school I was forced to ride my bike, down the sidewalk, through the lot, up the alley, down the street over and over again. Until one day, boom! My knee popped back into place, and I rejoiced that finally, I could walk normally again! That begins my acceptance of defining normal, recovering from the pain a man had given me.

So it was no surprise that I would end up in a battered woman's shelter after having a baby stomped from my body.

It was another fight on top of the endless battles. What is one more punch or slap when you are pregnant? How could I value the life growing in my belly when I didn't even appreciate my own? I do not write this blog as if I am innocent. I gave as good as I got. All I knew was fighting and dysfunction. I hit, he hit back, He hit, I hit back. He kicked. I didn't kick back. I clutched my stomach as I lay on the floor feeling life go from me. I slept in my daughter's bed that night. I remember she had sheets with some Disney character she liked on them. When I awoke, I noticed that blood had filled her twin bed sheets. She slept silently next to me oblivious to the fact that her brother or sister had just been expelled from my body. I moved her so she wouldn't be covered in blood. So much blood. A child that didn't need to be born in this world of chaos that I had created. I felt sad for me but happy for the child that never was. That baby deserved better. Perhaps the Universe reabsorbs innocent souls and sends to a family that is more deserving. Evidently, I wasn't worthy. My life was one big mess of confusion, drama, pain, and heartache. I was stunned the Universe saw fit to give me a daughter in the first place; surely it knew not to give me another child. So I absorbed that pain but resolved to leave that day. It was my 21st birthday when I found myself sleeping on the floor of my best friend's apartment. I couldn't stay there. I never wanted to be a burden on anyone. I called around and found a shelter that could take me and my daughter. This was only temporary. Right?

Temporary turned into a month and another month into two. It was the second month that I was walking through the common space when the payphone rang. I don't know why I picked it up, but I did.

"Hello."

"Hannah"

I froze. My heartbeat went from calm to chaotic seconds. "Dad?" I asked. I hadn't heard his voice in years, but I knew it.

"Yeah."
"How did you know I was here?"

"Your mom told me." I froze. My mom told him? My mother who knew I was in a shelter with her only granddaughter but didn't open up her home to me. My mom that turned her back on me for reasons I would never understand until I was older.

I was silent. I didn't know what to say. He did. "Come home."

I had nowhere else to go. My life was spiraling fast. So I hopped a Greyhound and said goodbye to the only place I ever called home and headed to Kentucky.

The road was long, traveling through states by bus that didn't have anything but flatland, fields, grass, and corn. I thought I would go delirious but then I made my way across the Ohio River, a few more stops and I would be home. I didn't know what that meant. Home to what? I had left chaos and wondered if I was traveling to more confusion. I got off the bus expecting a ticker tape parade. There was none. There were no reality TV tearjerker reunions. It was matter of fact. Was I home?

I looked at the man that had terrorized me my entire childhood. He looked the same only I was bigger, smarter, wiser. I would not tolerate his abuse. But he had none to dish out. He had changed. Made peace with his past. But I hadn't. I was angry, and I wanted him to hear me. He did. He didn't respond how I wanted only saying that God had forgiven him. Who gave a damn? I didn't forgive him. I stayed at his house for a few weeks before leaving to stay with my brother. I couldn't be in his home. He didn't understand me. He didn't realize what he had done to me, how the abuse had altered who I was as a human being and the course that was designed for my life. He couldn't get off that easy by invoking forgiveness. Fuck forgiveness.

-SELAH- PAUSE-

This
Has
Been
A
Long
Time
Coming
Suppressed Anger on a Crash Course with Fate
My past in a direct head on collision with my future
Do not pump the brakes!!
Here…there is no need for emotional air bags
This I have been expecting
I have seen this before,
Premonitions of the day that muted muffles would no longer remain silent
An accident waiting to happen
I brace myself, ready to face myself…ready to face…you
Skillfully maneuvering my words
A renowned poet and author
Four years studying Communication
A proud member of Eta Phi
And yet…the words…elude me
So I grasp, cling, clutch onto alphabetized apologies
And yet, I can only come up with….
DAD, FUCK YOU!
And still that just does not seem to sum up the way that I feel
So let me pause and make this clear for you so that I can begin to see
(Selah)
You…you made my life a living hell
In child like curiosity I did not need to wonder if monsters existed
Because the reality was I faced one every single day
Flesh ripped and oozing blood
Bones dislocated
Self esteem devastated
Beaten into submission
The person I was designed to be
Forever altered by iron fists that you swung
And even then in your anger you could not see
Blinded
The first kiss I ever shared was with your friend
Me a child and him a man
My mouth still reeks of the foul stench of tainted saliva
That invaded 11 year old lips open in shock
While you sat downstairs

I stood in pink painted rooms
Branded with the word whore
A label that clung to my being like pus oozing from a sore
And each time I spread my legs I just kept picking at the scab
And while I was fucking I thought FUCK YOU DAD!
You made me WHO I AM!
THIS HAS BEEN A LONG TIME COMING!!
So I wanted to talk about it, get it all on the table
And you…you give me SOME BULLSHIT about God's forgiveness
AND YES, HE DOES FORGIVE BUT FIRST YOU MUST REPENT!
SO BOW DOWN
Just say that you are sorry for making my life
A PIECE OF FUCKED UP SHIT WITH A FOUL STENCH
That EVERYONE could smell
Sorrow and heartache tinged with the scent of LIVING IN HELL
I'm ready to get it out
Let it go
Move on
But before I can say I love you I have to say FUCK YOU FOR BEING YOU
And for everything that you did
And FUCK YOU for never letting me be a kid
I WAIT… for the day… that you can TRULY say, I…AM… sorry.
THIS… HAS BEEN A LONG TIME COMING!!

But slowly I started to turn. I wanted my daughter to have a relationship with his man that I never knew. Watching him interact with her was like watching a stranger. I remember my daughter did something and I yelled at her at his house, and he told me, "Don't yell. Be gentle." I was stunned into silence. *Be gentle?* I never got that when I was a child but it made me reevaluate how I interacted with my daughter. I was always so hard, abrasive, coarse. I was who I had been conditioned to be. But when you know better you do better and this man that had made my life hell was challenging me to do better as a parent so I did. Slowly. As much as I didn't want to admit that I was him, it was him staring back at me in the mirrors and shadows as I yelled at my daughter, humiliated her and spanked her. I wish I could take those years back but didn't know any better. I just did what was my normal. And this man that was my monster was showing me a new normal.

My daughter gravitated to him, spent days and nights at his house, ate pizza rolls and snuck him candy bars which he shouldn't have had because of his weight. My daughter didn't care. That was her Poppa Daddy as she called him.

They were inseparable. They grew tomatoes together, she would water the plants as he looked on. They laughed and watched movies together. When he got sick and needed a trach and oxygen, she learned how to work his oxygen tank. They were pals. Then one day I was out of town, and he asked me to come get her. I raced home and snatched her up. She would not be made to feel like an inconvenience. Perhaps he was not feeling well that day and just not wanting company. Before we could get into the house, he called asking me to bring her back. I never did. That was the last day my daughter ever stayed the night with her Poppa Daddy. It was my baggage in the way of letting them continue their relationship. Perhaps baggage and fear that she would be made to feel insignificant like I had as a child and I wanted to protect her. But now I understand I kept her from spending time with someone that had so much to give that life didn't allow to give until it was ready. That is how life does. It swallows you whole and regurgitates you when it is ready. But you have to go through the yucky part first.

I didn't know that.

We still visited him at home. He had a curio cabinet filled with copper pots that he cherished, and no one could touch. He called me to his house one day and said, "Go back there and divide the copper pots between you and your sister." I did, and I said, "I will not cook in them and will display them in my house."

"Don't take them if you won't cook in them," he said.

He was still finding ways to shock me. He treated those pans in the curio cabinet like they were gold but now he regarded them as nothing but cookware. There was something in the way that he said don't take them that resonated with me. Everything he was had passed away. He was a new person. He chose a different path. He was a caterpillar that had transformed into a butterfly in front of my eyes.

I didn't forget my childhood. How could I? But I wanted to know this man that I never knew. And not long after I made that decision, he was gone. There are so many things I wanted to ask him. So many things I wanted to know. His last days were quiet. I spent them in the hospital with him. It was a Friday. I left him to spend the weekend with a friend. I told him that I would be back Sunday. Sunday never came. He died just hours after I said goodbye. And I wept for him. I missed him. Missed the Dad I never knew. There is a song by Reba McEntire I listen to often called The Greatest Man I Never Knew that reminds me of him. He was the greatest man I never knew.

His friend made a documentary about life. I didn't know my father had a life worthy of a documentary, but he did. I popped the disc into the DVD player one night with a glass of wine and watched him. He was a ghost dancing across my TV. And he told stories of his life, stories I never heard, stories that made me laugh, stories that made me cry, stories that made me long for a dad that I only knew a short while. In one moment on the TV screen, I heard him say, "My ex-wife did the best thing she could do and that was to get away from me and she should have did it a long time ago. She shouldn't have waited 20 years. I made her life miserable. I was miserable and my kids were probably miserable." My dad goes on to say, "My whole life has been one as an abuser." Pause. There it was. Something I had been seeking for years. Acknowledgment that he didn't give until years later. Yes, I was miserable and who I was as a person had already been formed, carved out to melt into walls in this misery. My existence was one to fade away, not be seen, take up the least space. But I was learning that it was okay to take up space, to exist, to be, to let the world know that I am here.

There was an incident at work that placed me back in that role as the little girl, abused by men in power that condone and punish women for a man's bad behavior. And that day I quit. I wasn't that little girl anymore. I didn't have to and wouldn't tolerate being chastised because a man wanted to abuse me and I walked away. And when I looked back, I saw so many memories down that road, memories I longed to forget all came springing up like flowers from the earth and somehow I knew my father in his transformation would be proud of me and would tell me, "Hannah, keep walking." So I did.

The greatest man I never knew lived just down the hall,
and ev'ry day we said hello but never touched at all.
He was in his paper. I was in my room.
How was I to know he thought I hung the moon?*

Change comes in many forms and happens in people we may never expect. I did not know XXXtentacion. I read of his deeds. Deeds that brought back far too many memories. I watched the back and forth on social media in the aftermath of his death. I understand the struggle of loving and hating someone that hurt you. The tug of war that takes place with your mind and your heart, the rational battling the irrational. I do not make any excuses for XXXtentacion's behavior. Truth be told, I do not even know his work to be a fan and this is his memory's cross to bear. I don't know why I read the article about him, what drew me to it. I do not understand why his death saddened me. Perhaps it's because I saw my father in him. A broken man, that broke others along his road to redemption. The only difference was that my father had time to change and I had time and the desire to forgive.

The greatest words I never heard I guess I'll never hear.
The man I thought could never die has been dead almost a year.

Oh, he was good at bus'ness but there was bus'ness left to do.
He never said he loved me. Guess he thought I knew...[1]

Love

(2): attraction based on sexual desire : affection and tenderness felt by
lovers After all these years, they are still very much in *love*.

LOVE, REVOLUTION & LEMONADE

God even loves women that have sex. Shug Avery told me so.

I don't think I ever really learned how to love someone.

Most of my relationships were based in chaos.

I always wanted to stay ahead of a someone hurting me so I ruined relationships before they could become relationships or I refused to commit or cheated.

I was searching for something that I still haven't found.

But I came close to love one time and it was beautiful.

THE BEST PART OF ME IS LAYING ON A MATTRESS

A young woman took the microphone, and her voice was so extraordinarily distinctive I paused. "Who is she?" I whispered to my friend sitting next to me. "Her name is Kendra." Her voice had a raspy, deep-throated tone that reminded me of singers in smoke-filled corner bars. Unassuming, yet when they belted out their first note the entire room stood still. That night the room paused, and I wondered how I did not know that I had been sitting in the presence of someone on the precipice of greatness?

I was already enchanted, and then Kendra sang a song that touched a part of my soul that had been hidden from many, at times, even me. I cannot recall the lyrics, but I do remember the chorus, "The best part of me is laying on a mattress". Her song was lighthearted but like most writers, I keyed in on that one phrase, and I could not shake it. I felt it soul deep as I wondered how many pieces of me, the best parts of me did I leave laying on a mattress?

Even as I write this, I find it difficult not to get emotional, remembering cheap hotels, five-star hotels, Egyptian cotton sheets, faded stained sheets, wondering why and how I ended up in these rooms, these places? Even more, when the room is a familiar place, where you rest your head nightly, and still you wonder how in your own home, you have left the best parts of who you are as a woman, on a mattress? I remembered as she sang, nearly 20 years earlier, lying in bed with my daughter after a physical altercation with an ex and waking up in a pool of blood. My body shedding a new life, before its time, from my womb on my daughter's twin size sheets. A womb that refused to hold a baby after being rocked by violence. And why would it want to be birthed into my chaos? My daughter, just 3, was oblivious to the blood that pooled around her. On that mattress, I left life.

Thinking now, I know some places I would never go again. Places I no longer desire to revisit. So many years have passed that they almost seem foreign to me. That life was another lifetime. Who I was then, I am not now, and I wondered what was lacking in me, what had I not received, what was going on inside of me that the best parts of me I left laying on a mattress?

As she sings, I accessed the feelings running rampant in my mind. Flashes of men, memories, missteps, misery, mistakes. I blanketed myself in sheets of shame, deep-rooted fear, memories of a little girl with innocence stolen. I thought about the time. So much time thrown away on a mattress with men that did not know me and never would. Never cared to. And I never bothered to make them care.

So much time. Wasted. Time that I wish I could collect again…yet it slips through my fingers as if I am attempting to gather grains of sand.

I wondered what were the best parts of me that I left laying on a mattress? It hurt to answer that question. In harsh honesty, I left my worth, my love, my self-esteem, my humor, my wit. I left my promise, my ambitions, my dreams. I left life in pools of blood. I left my inner me; that secret sacred me. I left the woman I was becoming. Left it on mattresses, along with conjured up moans and squeals, false promises and I love you's moaned on deceitful whispers. I left who I was among wrinkled sheets, discarded thongs and Trojan wrappers.

I left so much of me behind that it seems it has taken a lifetime for me to collect the pieces of me again. And still I find myself trying to find fragments of me discarded on mattresses from years ago. I refuse to believe that the best parts of me I have left behind in hotel rooms boasting rates by the hour, elegant hotel rooms with room service and even my room…my room…my home. There is more to me, so I find myself in my mind, collecting those pieces, and placing them back together again knowing one day, someday, I will be whole.

TEUSCHER CHOCOLATE

I still remember him like it was yesterday. Who could forget six feet and four inches of nothing but divine chocolate. Hershey had nothing on him. He was Teuscher champagne truffles, hand crafted by God. His skin was flawless. Muscles exuding from places I didn't even know muscles existed. After months of anticipation, finally, he stood in front of me. Live and in the flesh. Flesh that my mouth was waiting to devour.

We met over internet waves and poetry. Long before dating online was the norm, we set the norm. Keyboards conversations and long distance phone calls. He wrote haikus on my heart and I wrote soliloquies in the crevices of his soul. He was my anticipation in the flesh. We felt we had met in another lifetime, crossed paths with stolen glances and now life had aligned we were taking up the same space. My space was now our space and he felt right. Made my home a home until he made it hell. For a moment, everything was perfect but it easy for things to be perfect when you pretend you don't see.

I once heard someone say, "The worst kind of liar is someone that lies to themselves." And I was the worst kind of liar. I hid untruths and dislike underneath wheat bread, vegan cheese and faux mayo sandwiches. Always cut in half because that is what good wives do. They cut their husbands sandwiches in half, pack barbeque flavored chips and coconut water in brown bags along with notes about devotion and love written in perfect cursive. He was the perfect husband until he wasn't. I was the perfect wife. Until I wasn't.

I don't recall when I fell out of love. It was almost as ambiguous as the moment that I tripped and landed heart first in love. Or perhaps I fell in lust. I have asked myself this question a million times and still haven't landed on the correct answer. I would like to think that I was smarter than that but the heart wants what it wants and desire will always fight to be fulfilled. I do not think it was one thing that he did it was just a moment of everything, when he became everything, all consuming and the space that we shared was now overwhelmed with his books, tennis shoes, sandals, food, thoughts, opinions and words. Until there was no space left in the space for me to breathe. I was suffocating daily, fighting for air and no one around me offered any rescue breathing. As I look back I find it strange that I could be going through hell and those that claim to love me and care for the most were oblivious to the struggles that I was facing. Some people that claim they love you, never truly see you. They love you to the point of your use. And my use was always excellent because I was used to people using me.

Even him. Perhaps the day that I came home from a long day at work and found him reclining a bathtub that was too small for his limbs with bubbles was the day that I decided I had enough. The last time I reclined in a bubble bath was too far back for me to remember because responsibilities often don't move out of the way for moments of leisure. I didn't say anything as I opened the door to the bathroom. Just closed the door back and replayed the scene from Disappearing Acts when Sanaa Lathon's character walked to her front door, pulled out her keys to place them in the lock, thought about the pot of hell that was boiling over behind the door and turned and walked back down the stairs. Life was imitating art. Maybe that was the moment, when I saw that I was working for everything and he was hell-bent on consuming everything.

I remember my sister told me that a woman will get with a man and allow a man to be no good for her and she will go downhill and he will move on, better, stronger to the next woman. I found her words to be true. I was going downhill quickly. He ignited every vice that was in my lineage. Vices that remained dormant for generations only to rear their head when they came to me. Food, alcohol, smoking. If it could kill me, I was ready to consume it. Stopping only at drugs because I didn't, "like to feel weird." My extent with drugs was weed and mushrooms in college that didn't do a damn thing for me but I lied and pretended the 4th of July fireworks were damn near popping out of my eyelids. For all I know we were eating sautéed and dried portabellas.

I was not a "drug" girl and weed was too labor intensive. Light the incense, stop up the door, spate the stems and seeds, split the blunt, get fancy and show your man you can make a honey blunt, spray your clothes down with air fresher, risk the police getting involved. Who has the time? I'd rather my vices be bought legally and consumed in secrecy. But you cannot hide secrets from your home. My home knew the truth. Wanted me to let him go so the walls could exhale, so the curtains could breathe again, so the dishes could take a break from crashing to the floor.

It is funny how I love you can so easily turn to I hate you and I need you so easily turn to I never needed you. My resentment for him increased as any feelings to recognize his humanity decreased. I was not in the saving business once I recognized that it was I that was drowning.

I resented him now for the 2,102,400 minutes that he lingered in my space. Tick tock. Tick tock. We spent a fourth of those moments fucking, another fourth fucking to make up from our bullshit and the rest of the time wondering why we were continuing to put each other through this hell.

Some people enjoy wallowing in their pain. Perhaps I was addicted to him and him to me. He this six foot four chocolate tower that was melting before my eyes. Sweetness never tasted so bitter on my tongue but I tried as I knelt before him and consumed soul aching acidity. The submission of taking a dick in your mouth for his pleasure and your anguish is not arousing and takes more willpower than many men will understand when everything in your being is telling you even on your knees you can weaken him beyond any thought of his masculinity. Please do not be mistaken, a woman kneeling before a man is not a woman in submission but a woman in a position of dominance. Society certainly has the power of blowjobs confused. Perhaps we were both confused in our break up to make up dance.

Hold Up. You see, he didn't understand me. I didn't understand me and I was certainly in no position to understand him. What was I to do with a man that I had grown tired of like shoes hidden in the back of my closet? I was not lovable. And certainly, in no position to love. My love was fleeting. My love was like the wind.

He didn't know how to love me and I didn't know how to love him. I was never taught how to love. We didn't speak each other's love language so everything came out like a foreign language that neither of us understood. The only language that did make sense was in the bedroom and once that was destroyed we walked around the house mute. It is funny how loud silence spoke and how loud the walls shouted.

I didn't want him in my space anymore. The couch became his bedroom and my bedroom became my sanctuary. Some nights we decided, when hell had gone from inferno to unbearable, we could reside in the same space. We didn't understand how to be in the same space without obligatory fucking. That is what husband and wife do. Or maybe not. Maybe husband and wife make love. We were fucking, trying to mask it as love. That is what we understood.

Life is not without its irony. Out of despise can come rainbows. Red, Orange, Yellow, Green, Blue, Indigo, and Violet embedded in my womb. I carried the rainbow after the rain. I was a Black woman that danced in the rain and won, hair wet and all. Perhaps this is what it was all about. Bringing a life into this world.

But he doubted the rainbow. Denied the rainbow. His denial of the rainbow made me question everything. I could see my future passing before my eyes. I had played this single mother tune before, sang the melody, did the two step. Been there, done that. The weight of doing it again was like a vice grip on my womb.

My body had become a tomb. Me and my rainbow were the walking dead…

AN IDEA

He fell in love with the idea of me
Because it is easy to fall in love with ideas
The idea of loving someone is simple
Ideas don't talk back or make a fuss
Don't yell or get pregnant unexpectedly

Ideas don't break or bruise
Ideas don't fall out of love
Ideas are contained in the mind
Only causing trouble when they are put into action
Unleashed
Promiscuous

He didn't fall in love with the me that was roaming free
The me that felt like I could dip my hands into the soil and pull out
my ancestor's memories
The me that walked on my tiptoes to grasp handfuls of the sky
The me that believed I could contain lightening bugs, stars and clouds in a jar
The me that walked like I was creating canyons with every footstep

I was a shout in a crowd filled with whispers
And ideas ain't supposed to be loud
Ain't supposed to think out loud
His idea of loving me was putting me on a shelf
Locking me in a gilded cage where I could spin gold for my supper
Scribe soliloquies for my emancipation
Each journal entry I scribbled was my freedom papers
He never imagined that I would write myself to freedom
The very thing that united us would be the thing I used to divide us
Because ideas ain't supposed to be contained
Can't be contained
Won't be contained
And the idea of me will often stand toe to toe and do ten rounds with the real
me

What you see on stages is what is on stages
Please know that homes don't have spotlights
And bedrooms don't have microphones
Reality is not a Facebook post that can be edited
And life isn't neatly crafted in 280 characters

My life does not come with filters and headbands of floral bouquets

Truthfully, I am just a woman that is trying to navigate and make sense of it all
Trying to click my red heels without Louboutin bottoms in a tornado and write until I find home
Amongst men made out of straw, men without heart and those without courage
Courage enough to allow me to come down off the shelf
And just be me
Loud, irritable, happy, frustrated, sad
A bitch when I am on the rag

I drink too much wine and I whine too much
I want you close but far enough away that I can breathe
Inhale…exhale…inhale…exhale

I begged for space to just be
But my space crowded your idea of me
Took your idea of me and wrapped its fingers around the throat of unconditional love
Until you gasped for breath and conditions
Because unconditional love will always fight for conditions

But know that those enslaved will always fight for freedom
Since you didn't want to give me freedom
I took it
Hitched my soul, my pen, my paper to underground railroad trains
And rode into the land that Harriet spoke of,
"I had crossed the line. I was free; but there was no one to welcome me to the land of freedom. I was a stranger in a strange land."
A stranger in a strange land
Fighting to find my place among the weeds, and hope, and an idea that was manifested…

UNASHAMED

I wish I could say I loved the way he loved me
But I didn't
I loved all the ways he didn't love me
Maybe that's why his love was convenient
He required nothing from me
And I required nothing from him
He was just someone to fill the empty spaces
So he did

~

He entered me slowly
One... inch... at a... time
"Don't move."
I loved the way he could control me with so few words
I moaned softly.
"Where I am," he asked as pushed inside of me deeper
"Fear."
"I'm going to go deeper. Tell me where am I now?"
"Pain."
"Uh huh. How about now?"
"Shame."
"Have I reached it yet?"
"No."
"Where am I now, Hannah?"
"Hurt."
It was all there
All Buried
I fought back tears
I didn't know why all those words tumbled out of my mouth
In my nakedness, I was naked before him
And I realized that my pleasure no longer had to be connected to my pain
"Have I found it yet, Hannah?"
"Yes."
"Tell me where I am?"
" In me. All of me."
"Now, let's make love."
And for the first time in a long time
I wasn't ashamed...

This world tries to tell women who they can be sexually. If you are strong and powerful the world tells you that you cannot be sexy… but powerful women are sexy. If you are fighting for liberation and justice that is sexy. If you are on the front lines of the revolution that is sexy.

I am tired of people telling me who and what I can be.

I am a woman that screams, "No justice. No peace," and I can go home and scream, "Fuck me harder."

Women can be all things. We are sexual beings that do not need to be afraid of our passion and desires. We no longer need to feel ashamed for the fire in our bellies or in between our thighs.

FUCK

With my brown bag and champagne flute demeanor
He must have gotten beside himself
and thought I was one of those "around-the-way" girls
When he said "fuck" to me in a way that made me have flashbacks
of childhoods spent hiding in corner shadows
Flashbacks of a man that said he loved me
and punctuated his love with fisticuffs that screamed fuck you
Flashbacks of stolen innocence
All summed up in one word-F.U.C.K.
So before we go any further

Let's be crystal clear
This is how you can use the word fuck in the presence of excellence:
Fuck me harder.
Fuck me faster.
Do you like how I am fucking you?
Do you want me to fuck you deeper?
I am gonna fuck the shit out of you.
Oh fuck, your pussy feels so fucking good,
Fuck me baby!
Oh fuck, I'm cumming.
I am so fucking crazy about you.
You fuck me so good
You are so fucking sexy.
I am a lucky fucking man!
I have never been fucked like this before!
I love fucking you!
I fucking love you…
Those are all options.

Take note:
Fried bologna sandwiches on wheat bread with mayo and hot sauce
or
Beluga caviar served on top of blini
Never forget when you speak to me
I am always a fucking lady!

DANCE FOR ME

"Bravo! Bravo! Marvelous job! How many curtain calls was that tonight? Two? Three?"

"I wasn't keeping count," Deanna softly said as she sat at her table in her room backstage. The lights around the mirror reflected off her face. Any other time she would be gushing with pride, tonight she noticed that her eyes had lost that special glow she would feel after such a stellar performance. It has been three nights of her starring in the hit Broadway show, Lights on Fire. Each night she managed to bring the house down. Each night she felt even more alone. She was 25 and living her dream. At least what she believed to be her dream. Most ballerinas didn't last to see her age, but a star was a star and even age couldn't deny fame. The lines had become blurred many years ago between what her mother wanted and what she wanted. At three years old she had no choice but to be dragged to dance class. Dance came easy for her and she moved up the ranks swiftly. Tap, jazz, contemporary, hip-hop but it was ballet in which she excelled. As her first instructor put it, it was if Deanna was gliding through the air, not dancing but seeming to float effortlessly across the floor, to a melody that could not be heard with the ears but only felt with the soul.

"Oh you silly girl. I would lose count after four curtain calls myself. The applause, the roses at your feet. Why I haven't seen audiences respond like that since I watched Tai Jimenezin. What year was that? Oh who cares, you were simply marvelous, Deanna."

Deanna forced a smile as she glanced up at her agent. It had been a year since they had attempted to date. Awkward was not the word to describe it. Painfully uneasy would be better. She was used to Miles being confident and sure of himself as he negotiated on her behalf as a guest ballerina that performed all around the world, however sitting across from her in a restaurant; he seemed almost in disbelief that he was actually dining with her. She could tell from the way he stared at her, she was not Deanna the woman. She would always be Deanna the ballerina to him and for her that meant it could never work. In addition to that, she could hear her mother's disapproval if she told her she was dating her agent. 'How trite and unbelievably mediocre and common that my daughter a principal ballerina would be slumming it with her agent'. It was common. And Deanna was never allowed to do anything common. Climb trees? No, she could break a leg. Run? Most certainly not. Bad for the feet. Sleep with a man that manages you? Not a chance in hell. It would soil her name, her brand and she would just be one of those girls, who managed to screw their way through Julliard or the New York Ballet Company, who had sickled feet and whose only claim to fame was giving a good blowjob to the director of some far off Broadway production. Deanna was better than that. She had worked her entire life for this moment. Deanna joined the NYC Ballet at age 18 and was a professional dancer for more than ten years. She performed with the NYC ballet for eight years dancing numerous soloist and principal roles before she decided to leave the company. Deanna joined the legendary Bejart Ballet, in Lausanne, Switzerland. And after successful touring Europe, she returned to the United States as a freelance ballerina. She spent her time touring and even entertained the idea of teaching once she retired.

Deanna was ready to find something or someone to entertain her. She had no children, her father spent most his time working overseas and her mother still acted as she was a stage mom still vying for her daughter to get the lead in some dance recital. Outside of the date, if she would even call it that with Miles, she hadn't been out in years. Most men in her field batted for the other team and those that didn't believed they were God's gift to women. Most nights after a performance so fraught with applause and accolades, she spent the evening at home, alone, eating something sinfully delicious that was often on her lists of no's. Wine? No. Cheesecake? No. Fries? Not a chance. For the last ten years of her life her meals consisted of a salad with no dressing, brown rice and roasted chicken breast. There was only so many ways she could try to dress up the mundane.

Perhaps that is why she went to Illicit in the first place. Because she just needed something different. Something to give her that spark back in her eyes. She knew enough people in the entertainment world that had secrets. That made sure their escapades didn't find their way on to the cover of The National Enquirer or breaking news on Entertainment Tonight. With enough money, anything could always be hidden. Once she started to tour the world and dance for men of stature, her rates increased. She had never been a starving artist. Financially, Deanna had everything that she desired. It also helped that her father established a trust fund for her years ago. He assumed money would make up for his lack of time and attention. It never did so she invested well and lived a simple life and that's why when she was handed the black card with Illicit embossed across the front in unassuming font along with a telephone number she didn't blink an eye when given the amount for her fantasy. She was assured it would be worth every penny. After the financial aspect had been taken care of, the meeting was very simple. Deanna completed some forms detailing her most intimate desires, things she had never shared with anyone. Things she was too embarrassed to say out loud. Seeing her words on paper made it all too real. This was happening.

She didn't know when it would happen. She didn't want to. She was afraid if she knew she would back out. Tell them to just keep the money and forget she had ever made the phone call. Her only instruction was that she wanted to be surprised. Caught off guard. That way she knew she would go through with it. The person on the other end of the line assured her that she would personally handle all the details for her venture as she so eloquently put it. All she needed to know was when Deanna would be in town, her hotel information and her itinerary for the weekend. Once these things were supplied Deanna put the phone call out of her mind and continued with her life as if she never made the call.

"Deanna, did you hear me?"

Deanna continued wiping her face with the satin cloth removing the stage makeup from her face. Underneath all the eyeliner and lashes she was even more stunning. A natural beauty. Her skin looked flawless underneath the lights, rivaling smooth homemade caramel- like a mixture of brown sugar and heavy cream, simmered to perfection. Her hazel eyes were wide set, almost doe-like and innocent. However, if anyone looked closely beyond the innocence, they could see the clear glint of a mischievous personality. She was almost mesmerizing just to gaze upon let alone to watch dance.

"I'm sorry, Miles. What did you say?"

"Your guests."

"My guests?" Deanna was confused.

"Goodness, Deanna where is your head tonight? The meet and greet."

Deanna sighed loudly. She was not in the mood to be on display anymore tonight. She had just given her soul to them with every sautes, soubresauts, echappe, pas assemblé jete, and now they wanted more.

"Miles…" Just as she was about to object, a knock came to the door.

"Come in."

"Hello. I have a delivery for Miss Sweeting." Deanna glanced at the delivery man. He was dressed in a suit and tie not the standard khaki attire for someone in his position.

""Please come in."

"You were excellent tonight, Ms. Sweeting."

"Thank you. Did you watch the show?

"Yes…yes I did. It's rare that get to see the ballet. My daughter…she dances. Not anything like you, of course but she's well on her way."

"Please, next time I am in town contact Miles and he will get you tickets to the show."

Miles rolled his eyes. "We really don't have time for you to be conversing with the delivery boy, Deanna."

"Miles please. People like, I'm sorry, I didn't get your name?"

"Frederick."

"Thank you. People like Frederick are my real guests. Not some pompous, pretentious assholes that donated a few dollars to their local Arts Center and are looking for some big tax write off. How many more glasses of champagne can I pretend to drink with people that only enjoy me for a few moments?"

"Goodness, Deanna. Do you know how hard I work?"

"Yes, yes I do, Miles. The question is, do you know how hard I work?"

"I've practically made your name a household name. When people think of ballet you are right up there with the greats and pretending to sip a few glasses of champagne with people that donate thousands of dollars to the arts is not very much to ask of you."

"If you don't mind, Miss Sweeting, I should go. He is correct. I did not come for tickets. I came to drop off your package. I shouldn't have mentioned my daughter.

Forgive me. My job is to be easily forgotten. It was wonderful meeting you. Please tend to your fans." With that he turned and left, closing the door behind him.

"Really, Miles?"

"What? I don't like for you to waste your time on people that have no interest in advancing you as a dancer. This is not some corner store dance studio for goodness sake! We have patrons that love you and that are willing to finance you having your own school, starting your own company. The world is yours right now, Deanna. Anything you could want or even imagine. We don't have any time to waste on a delivery boy and his daughter getting tickets."

Deanna didn't feel like arguing tonight. She turned her attention to the small box wrapped in plain brown paper. The gold seal that held the package together was simply marked 'I.E.'

And so it begins.

The nerves she normally felt before a big show were nothing in comparison to what she was feeling now as she ran her fingernail underneath the seal and broke it. "Can you please excuse me, Miles." She didn't know what was in the box and in her mind she conjured up the most embarrassing items. The last thing she needed was for Miles to know that she was still a woman and thought about more things than just pirouettes and pliés.

"Five minutes, Deanna."

"Sure. Five minutes," Deanna managed to muster as Miles walked out of her dressing room. Her focus was no longer on Miles but on the box. She closed her eyes and took a deep breath. She knew once she removed the plain wrapper from the box and examined the contents there would be no turning back. But this is what she wanted. What she needed. She opened her eyes as she slowly pulled the wrapping down to reveal an ornate, wooden music box. She could tell from the way it was carved that was handmade from the finest wood. It was a deep cherry wood and finished in a high gloss. It was almost so beautiful that Deanna was afraid to touch it. She reached up slowly and opened the top and instantly Brahms Lullaby begin to play as a small glass ballerina spun in time with the music. Deanna smiled. It has been years since she had seen a music box such as this however, never had she seen one on such a high-end scale. Inside the music box was folded linen piece of paper. She pulled it up and unfolded it. It was a simple question written on the inside in eloquent detail, "Are you ready to truly dance?" Yes, she wanted to scream as her heart beat heavy inside of her chest. Yes, she was ready to dance, to leap, to be free.

There is a car waiting for you outside. I look forward to dancing with you, Deanna. Always, Antonio.

Deanna looked in the mirror and noticed her cheeks were now flush. She grabbed the music box and her bag and headed out of the dressing room. Miles was standing waiting. "I have to go, Miles."

Go? What do you mean go? We have donors and sponsors and people you need to meet!"

"Tell them I hope they enjoyed the show"! Deanna yelled as she ran out the door to the black sedan that was waiting for her before Miles had a chance to object.

"Good evening, Miss. Sweeting."

"Good evening."

"My name is Charles. I've been instructed to take you back to your hotel. Take as much time as you need to prepare and I will be waiting for you once you are ready to leave."

He opened up the backseat of the sedan and Deanna slid in. On the seat was a small envelope. "The envelope will contain further instructions. Can I pour you a glass of Krug Rosé ?"

Deanna couldn't remember the last time she actually drink a glass of champagne. Too many calories. Her entire diet was bland and monochromatic. Just like her life. Bland. Tasteless. One note.

"No...wait...yes. I'm sorry.

"No need to apologize, ma'mm." He maneuvered in the car, parked, got out and quickly popped the cork and poured a glass of champagne in the Waterford crystal flute. Deanna was almost amazed at the high level of detail. She recognized the flutes from her mother's collection as well as the champagne. It was clear that Illicit had spared no expense.

"Enjoy ma'mm."

"Thank you, Charles. He hurried to the front of the car and drove through the downtown streets while Deanna sipped her champagne letting the bubbles dance on her tongue as she giggled like a school girl.

As she sipped she read the instructions contained in the envelope.

Deanna,

You must be overwhelmed with the all the applause and accolades. I am sure you believe that you were so mesmerizing that no one noticed your turns were just off center. And after the first act, you came back just a bit tired. Your jumps were not as high, your arabesque could use some work. But only someone trained in dance would notice those things. To the normal eye you were enchanting. To me, I am not that impressed. Tonight you will dance for me. Impress me, Deanna. Show me who you really are behind the leotards and the tutus. I want to see all of you. ~ Antonio

Deanna gulped her champagne as if it was a box wine. In all her years she had never heard anyone critique her so harshly. She was a perfectionist. She was always the best and now this man, someone she had never met, was analyzing her movements. Strangely, surprisingly, Deanna felt a slight tingle in between her thighs. Something about his criticism she found highly arousing. By the time Charles pulled in front of her hotel, she was now throbbing.

"I will be just a few moments."

"Take all the time you need, Miss Sweeting. I will be here waiting."

Deanna dashed from the car and made it to her room in record time. She looked over the contents of the list that she was to bring and then jumped in the shower

to refresh her body. She hopped out of the shower, lathered her body in lotion, tossed on a pair or skin tight jeans, tank top and slipped into her heels, grabbed everything she had been requested to bring and headed out the door.
~

"Thank you so much, Charles."
"It was my pleasure to drive you, Miss Sweeting. Enjoy your evening."
~

Deanna stood in front of a small building almost afraid to walk through the door. She didn't know what was on the other side. But her fear would not stop her. She was in too deep. There was no turning back. She opened up the door and walked inside of what appeared to be a small dance studio. The lights came on slowly as she entered. The floor was freshly buffed. She could smell the lemon scent lingering in the air. The fresh wax on the floor almost glowed underneath the lights. On one side of the room there were mirrors from the floor to the ceiling, the other side had a ballet barre.

He sat in the middle of the studio in a wooden folding chair. This cannot be real. It was almost unbelievable. This was the man that she had envisioned so many nights when she was alone. When there was no audience applause. He almost seemed too perfect. He wore a simple white tank top that contrasted beautifully against his skin. It was a shade that reminded Deanna of Brazilian Rosewood, a creamy mixture of reddish brown hues. He wore a slightly oversized New York Yankees baseball cap with the brim touching just below his eyebrows. His locs were twisted neatly with a hint of sheen in them and hung just to the tops of his wide shoulders. Deanna could feel drops of saliva building inside of her mouth. She swallowed hard as her eyes gazed over his body. His arms were well defined, hints of veins showing on his muscles. His chest filled out the thin material of the shirt. Even sitting down she could tell he stood well over 6 feet. His loose blue jeans fell just low enough over the cuff of his tan boots. He was the guy her mother had always warned her about. He was not the sophisticated ballet dancer. He was oozing masculinity and Deanna was ready to drink every last drop.

"Hello, Deanna."
Goodness she loved how her name sounded in his mouth.
"Hello, Antonio."
"You can change in there." He pointed to a small room just off to the side of the studio. "Don't keep me waiting."
"I wouldn't dare." Deanna said as she quickly made her way to the room to change her clothes.

He had requested that she wear a ballet costume. She chose an ornate costume from her lead role in La Esmeralda. It reminded her of peacock's feathers. It was an extremely decorative piece that was handcrafted for her and fit her body perfectly accentuating her slender waist when she pulled the crisscrossed strings of the bodice which was made of sparkling golden fabric and embellished with dangling sequins. The overlay was made of lace decorated with golden braid, appliqués and large sequins. For added elegance, crystals and golden glass beads are also used as décor elements on the tutu. It was simply stunning. Finally she slipped her feet into her satin pointe ballet slippers and glanced at herself in the mirror. She was ready for one of the biggest performances of her life for an audience of one.

As she stepped from the room she could feel his eyes on her. The lights in the room had dimmed and a single spotlight was in the center of the room. She felt foolish standing in front of him. Her she stood in an outfit styled by one of the top designers in the world, an outfit that ballerinas would kill to dance in and she felt silly. She seemed almost too perfect. Her makeup was flawless, her hair pulled back in a tight chignon. The juxtaposition of her perfection next to his casual street wear aroused her.

Rose Adagio by Tchaikovsky filled the room. It was a song she knew well. She had danced the lead in Sleeping Beauty years ago. "To the barre."

Deanna quickly moved across the room and placed her hand on the barre. He called out positions and she executed each one of them flawlessly.

"We know you know the moves, Deanna. It is rare that you will make a mistake." She nodded. "Now I want you to dance for me. Move your body for me. Dance for me like a whore would. Like you would, Deanna. That's what you want isn't it?"

"Yes," she replied softly.

Antonio walked up behind her and pulled her hair out of its tight bun and ran his infers through her hair. She gasped as his fingers touched her scalp, massaging it briefly before pulling her hair back. "Whores are not so well put together, Deanna."

She shook her auburn tresses out and ran her fingers through her hair. She liked this just a little bit too much. The music changed and the room was filled with Maxwell and Alicia Keys The Fire We Make. Deanna's hips instantly caught the rhythm and she gyrated her hips and moved her body sensually. Antonio caught her rhythm as he came up behind her, his hands sliding down her both sides of waist and to her hips pushing his manhood against the rise of her butt.

"This is how you long to dance." They glided across the room as two people not just dancing but making love to each rise and fall of the music." Do you know why men go to the ballet, Deanna?" he whispered in her ear.

"No," she said almost panting.

"Do you think it's because they just love the ballet?"

"I...I," she didn't know how to answer his question. Everything was jumbled in her head. Scenes of her entire dancing career flashed through her mind. None of it mattered. She would toss it all aside if she could feel like this every night.

Antonio ran his hands up her body over her breasts and cupped her right breast in his hand before ripping the bodice exposing her naked flesh. A small gasp escaped from her lips. She felt in between her legs clinch and then release. Her nipples were hard as he pulled the bodice down to her waist revealing her taut stomach and firm, perky breasts. He moved to the music and turned her away from him facing the mirrors. Deanna was almost too afraid to look at herself. "Open your eyes. This is you, Deanna. This is who you want to be." She looked at herself in the mirror. Her chest rising and falling, his hands flowing over her body. His hand ran down her stomach and cupped her pussy in his hand. "Men go to the ballet, Deanna so they can see a beautiful woman dancing in such a way that exposes this." He squeezed her pussy tighter and Deanna could feel her lips swell. "It's no different than a man going to a strip club, you just cost a little bit more." He tore her outfit further; the thin fabric seemed as if he was ripping paper in his hands. Before she could blink, she was stood naked in the mirrors with nothing on but her satin ballet slippers. "Every night you are on stage moving your body you are simply selling a fantasy. Do you how many men probably go home and fantasize about you and when they sleep with their wives they are probably imagining that beautiful black woman that spread her legs and flashed them a cute little glimpse of her plump pussy lips all while bending and contorting her body to classical music? The things they would love to do to you."

His words were making her wetter. She had never heard it put that way. She was the upper echelon of the dance world. She was better than the Michelle Ford's and Superheads of the world. Or so she thought before she entered this studio. Right now she was just another woman that was naked, willing, open and ready. "Pointe!"

Instantly she positioned her body and was on her toes.

"What man wouldn't want to have that?"

"Arabesque and hold position."

Her left leg lifted in the air and Antonio dropped to his knees and knelt beneath her, his full lips kissing her gently against her pussy, before sliding his tongue deep inside of her. It took every ounce of control for her to hold her position. His tongue slipped out and circled her clit. She couldn't hold the position any longer. Just as she was about to drop her leg, he lifted her as he stood, her legs over his shoulders, his mouth never leaving her pussy as he dined in between her legs. Deanna felt secure in his arms, his huge hands supporting her back as she moved in cadence with him. He pushed his tongue deeper inside of her and she exploded, her juices coating his tongue as he continued to eat her and swallow every drop of her juices.

After her shaking had subsided, he lifted and sat her down gracefully. "You taste just as I imagined you would, Deanna. Sweet, succulent, creamy." Deanna felt her cheeks grow hot. Now was not the time to be embarrassed. He quickly stripped out of his clothes and Deanna slowly took in every inch of his body. His stomach was rippled with muscles and his manhood was bigger than any she had ever seen—hard, thick, long, inviting. Deanna licked her lips as she moved to the music. He glided over to her and pressed her body against the mirror. "I want you to see everything, Deanna." He lifted her as if he was lifting her for an elaborate lift sequence and placed her right on the tip of his dick. "Now work your way down on me."

Deanna rolled her hips and could slowly feel her body adjust to his width. She had no idea how he was going to fit inside of her small frame but she was determined to make it work. His dick instantly filled every crevice of her pussy, pushing hard against that secret place that so many men struggled to find. He had no problems and she knew he didn't need her encouragement as he asked, "right there?" She could tell from the cockiness of his voice that he knew that he had found her spot. "Yes, Antonio, right there.

His dick slid in and out of her pussy, creating sounds she had never heard before. She had stopped hearing the music and only heard the rhythm of their intimacy, as his breath was heavy on her back and his hands pulled her up and down on his dick. "What do you want, Deanna?"

She didn't want to say. Not like this. Here she was a sought after ballerina that had danced on stages in Paris, Milan, London, New York's, Metropolitan Opera House and yet her she was reverse riding a man that looked as if he should be in the latest hip hop video rather than buried deep inside of her fucking her from behind.

"What do you want, Deanna?" he asked her again, this time more firmly as his hips stopped moving.

She stared in the mirror. She wanted to feel dirty. She wanted to feel like a whore. She wanted to feel like those strippers who shook their ass for a few crumbled dollar bills.

"Fuck me."

"Louder!"

Fuck me!" she screamed. The words seem to bounce off of the dance studio walls and echo in the small space.

She never stopped looking at herself.

There was no applause. No roses thrown at her feet. No curtain calls. Just him pounding her against the mirror as she moaned and groaned in fits of pleasure. She felt as if he was hitting every area inside of her and every area she longed to be touched. The curve of his dick fit perfectly inside of her body and she bucked her hips and rode him harder. He picked her up and placed her on the floor. There was no padding. No bearskin throws on the floor. No wall to wall cashmere carpeting. No luxury. Just her on her knees, his hand pushing against her back, positioning her ass up to him. Her face was down her, her nose smelling the wax on the floor as his fingers dug into her hips as he pulled her back onto him. She spread her legs wider allowing him complete entry. She wanted him in deeper. Maxwell's For Lovers Only filled the room. He moved in and out of her pussy to the beat of the music before laying his body down on top of her and slowing grinding his dick in her body as his fingers ran through her hair, pulling her hair and whispering against her ear, "You are such a slut, Deanna. Look at you. What would the audience think of you now?" She shivered as he spoke the words.

Imagining a crowded auditorium filled with patrons watching her in the throes of ecstasy. She didn't care any longer. She longed for them to watch, to applaud her for being such a wanton whore, to marvel at the way she could twirl her hips and squeeze her pussy until it engulfed his dick and slid back to her g-spot. With just that thought, she felt her juices gush over him and spill from inside of her onto the floor.

He was the choreographer of this scene. She was just a girl playing her part. She allowed her body to dance for him. Their hips moving in sync as she came over and over again, her body now sliding in the sweat and cum that dripped from both of them. She hadn't been fucked like this in years. Not even close and she loved every single moment of it. For her, she was on stage. She was finally performing as the woman she longed to be. The woman that lived deep inside of her. He pulled out and slammed it back inside of her one final time before rolling her over and entering her once again. Deanna looked up at him, his muscles bulging, his locs swaying with each thrust, the look in his eyes one of determination. He wanted to please her. To make her feel what she had been wanting, longing for. She wrapped her legs around his back and he slid his hands underneath her butt and pulled her down completely. "Ohhhhhh." Deanna moaned. Her back arched, her body shivered as she came one final time with Antonio's name on her lips. But he was not done. She was just a dancer in his show and he had not finished his finale. He thrust inside of her one last time. "Deanna," he moaned as he pulled his dick from inside of her and positioned himself over her body. Deanna held her head back and waited for his cum to splash her face or her breasts. She welcomed it. Instead, he moved down and dripped it all over her satin ballet shoes.

"A souvenir for your performance tomorrow night."

Deanna smiled up at him as she gazed at her shoes and the juices seeped inside the fabric.

No one would be able to see the stains under the glare of the stage lights. Only she could notice them if she looked up close. Only she would know they were there. As she danced in front of hundreds and they spoke in hushed tones about her grace and agility. The fact that she was so eloquent and refined, she would know that if only for one night, she danced for an audience of one.

To her own tune.

To her own beat.

To his rhythm.

I TAUGHT HIM THAT

The way he runs his tongue over your clit, I taught him that
The way he slides his tongue in and out of your pussy, I taught him that
The way he kisses your neck as he slides his 12 inches inside of you, I taught him that
The way he makes love to you and simultaneously fucks you, I taught him that
The way he makes you feel like a queen and his nasty whore, I taught him that

The way he scrambles your morning eggs with just a bit of heavy cream, I taught him that
The way he squeezes fresh oranges for you to have juice, I taught him that
The way he has learned to be attentive to the way you take your coffee, I taught him that

The way he prepares your bath water, not too hot and not too cold, but just right, I taught him that
The way he massages your feet after a long day, I taught him that
The way he caresses your hair not messing up one single track, I taught him that

The way he loves you like a man should love you, I taught him that
The way he allows to be vulnerable in his presence, I taught him that
The way he makes you moan, I taught him that

Every single thing you are enjoying about "your man," please know that he was the student and I was the professor
I taught him the beauty of knelling before the alter of my feminine wisdom
Everything that he knows, I taught him

And to my chagrin, who knew that I was preparing him for the next bitch…

I TAUGHT HER THAT

The way she knows to slide two fingers in your pussy and not just one, I
taught her that
The way she instinctively knows to suck your clit up and down, I taught her
that
The way she lightly grazes her teeth over your clit, giving you both pleasure
and pain, I taught her that
The way she slides her tongue in your pussy while pinching your nipples, I
taught her that
The way she knows to push deeper until she finds your G-spot, no references
needed, I taught her that
The way she fucks your pussy with a strap-on with poetic rhythm, I taught
her that
The way she flips you your stomach and takes you from behind, I taught her
that too

The way she lets you place your head in her lap while you watch TV, I taught
her that
The way she doesn't body shame you but worships your curves and runs her
tongue along your stretch marks, I taught her that
The way she finds a way to point out the beauty of your c-section scar, I
taught that
The way she massages your back, paying special attention to the stress you
carry in your shoulders, I taught her that
The way she says, "Mistress, I am here to please you," I taught her that
The way she serves you impeccably, I taught her that

The way she fries your bacon, I taught her that
The way she serves your grits, I taught her that
The way she butters your biscuit with a side of grape jelly, I taught her that

Every single thing you are enjoying about "your woman," please know that
she was a well-trained and dedicated intern
I taught her the beauty and liberation of serving a Black Queen
Everything that she knows, I taught her…EVERYTHING

And in spite of all that, I smile as she walks away knowing I was preparing
her for the next woman…

LICK ME

He wanted to lick me
Wanted to spread my legs
Lick me in places that I held sacred
Places that tasted like pineapples drizzled with honey

He wanted to lick me
Flip me on my stomach and trace his tongue up and down my spine
Lick me in places that many held taboo
And when he asked me, "Baby does that sound good to you?"

I didn't even blush because I was far from meek
And I told him,
"Sweetheart,
Boys lick.
Grown men, eat."

LOVE, SEX, AND REVOLUTION

As the stress from day in and day out activism piled up, the endless videos of #BBQ Becky's, mounted on top of police body cam footage released on social media showing the death of yet another Black victim, I wonder, "How can I deal with the stress that is creeping up the back of my thighs, settling in the base of my spine, snaking its way up my back and settling into my head with a dull rhythm that only oppression knows?" It is the daily assault of waking up each morning girding your Black humanity just to exist in White spaces, facing microaggressions and stupid questions like "Can I touch your hair," as if you are a part of a petting zoo, that slowly wear at you like an incessant drop of water on a rock. Day in. Day out. Day in and day out, as if you are doing time at Shawshank and sadly there is no clever Andy Dufresne with an escape route or Morgan Freeman to narrate the mundane bullshit.

And believe me, the bullshit is never-ending. When you are in it, you are in it, and it is often at the expense of you and your life. While I have always had a passion for Black people and our struggles, something clicked for me hard when Trayvon Martin was murdered. I could not just write a few poems about Black people and go on about my business. I felt intricately connected to what happened to Trayvon and from that moment on my life was consumed with justice for Black people. Everything that I thought was important to me went to the wayside. Any relationship made its way to the back burner in my life. I found myself too busy focused on fighting injustice than worrying about having sex. I didn't have the time to cultivate a serious relationship let alone a hookup. People were dying, and my needs as a woman didn't seem as important. It wasn't that I took the time to sit and think about it, it was just that I was so busy that I DIDN'T think about it at all. Until those late nights when I could feel the weight of days and months and years without any physical intimacy. In fact, the other day I was so physically stressed that I wondered why don't people just rage fuck to deal with all of this drama? No commitment. No stress. No worries. Just have sex for the sake of having sex and relieving stress and having a great time?

I've not had sex with someone in a long time where there were no thoughts of revolution between us. Just Googling Black men and women the images that popped up were telling. It seemed Google dedicated most of its images of Black men and women, to be images of us fighting or of Black men with White women.

Clearly that is the stereotype. Black men and women always seem to have an undercurrent of life pulsating beneath us that is determined to keep us perpetually apart and on the edge.

Even writing this I wonder is it possible for Black men and women, in whichever way that shakes out, just to enjoy one another sexually? Is it possible for us to set aside all the worries in the world and just exist together for a moment, or moments upon moments? Can we just be? Can we exist in each other's arms, can we lay together legs entangled, can his beard brush in between my thighs, as my fingertips run along the top of his head as I moan for him to lick me harder, faster, urging his tongue to go deeper just before he enters me? Making love, or making peace with each other because we just need a moment in this world to breathe and show one another that is okay to love, to feel, to be.

Siggghhhh, a girl can dream….

Those moments just don't seem to exist. And I wish they did!

I wondered why they didn't exist for me, so I asked my friend, Steven about love and sex and revolution, and he said, "Many men make the assumption that women like you have yourself together already and don't want anyone. You seem happy alone, and if not, you can have anyone you want instantly."
Goodness. Was my strength making me appear unapproachable? He told me, "Women must learn to speak up and demand what they want."

Fair enough. I believe that women can and should speak up and ask for what they want. The days of playing coy seem to be long over. But that still didn't address being a Black woman that is an activist that just wants to find love and sex all while fighting towards the revolution.

A Black woman can be on the front lines. A Black woman can be a fighter. A Black woman can be strong and powerful and demanding. And we can still desire love and intimacy, hot and raw and sticky, hair pulling, fuck me from the back sex then cuddle with me and run your fingers along my thighs and kiss the part of my neck that makes me moan, and let me feel that just for a moment it is going to be okay. Let me just breathe into you and you into me, let us just enjoy each other, with no thoughts of revolution between us.

I need to know that Black women can rest in the arms of Black men and women and feel safe. I need to know that not every Black man or woman is cheating and looking for the next best thing.

I need this world to know before there was ever 50 Shades of Grey there were 100 Shades of Black. I need to see that Black men and women can be passionate and erotic. I need to know that Black men still look at Black women like Barack looks at Michelle. I need to see that because I am that.

I am woman that loves, love and that loves intimacy and passion and all things kinky and erotic and discreet. And sometimes we need a break from the machine. A moment to pause, to exhale, to breathe deeply. To connect and moan and tingle in the arms of a lover. A time to just pause and to truly make love. The revolution will be there in the morning but right now…right now I need you and you need me in every way possible.

SEASONS OF JOY

There are times in your life that you can accept there will be Seasons of Joy.

She is my season.

I admired her from afar.

Watched the sun kiss her locs

Enamored by her smile

She took my breath away

Who was this woman that made me want to take a chance again?

I made a decision to love her unafraid…

…Even while I was afraid…

…Today you made me want to write
Haikus
Soliloquies
Sonnets
Today you made me want to
Create
Envision
Dream

Today you made me want to be
Great
Bold
Unapologetic
Today you made me want to
Love
Live
Dream…

CONTOURS & CURVES

I love the way her body fits next to mine
Like the perfect puzzle piece
It's as if the Universe molded her shape just for me
Her curves were my private dancer
Her body pressed against mine
In tune to the rhythm of our heartbeats
She was chiseled just for me and I for her
Our bodies were in sync
When she moved, she melted into the grooves of my hips
Her hand finding its home along the curve of my breasts
Our flesh connected without saying words
Mentally I trace the contours of her silhouette
I have studied every curve of her body
I was a student at the altar of her contrasting X & Y energy
Teach me…(Slower, Hannah.)
Show me… (Right there, Baby.)
School me…(I'm not going anywhere, Baby.)
Tell me…(Fuck me, Hannah.)
She is flawless…beauty wrapped in flesh
Each curve reminds me of undiscovered constellations
She allows me to discover her…explore…her
Unearth her longing…her wanting…her needs…
Her legs opening, inviting me in
This is where I belong
Her body beckons me with every moan
My fingertips along the small of back
Running down to the rise of hips
Her back arches
Her legs instinctively rest upon my shoulders
As my mouth engulfs her
My tongue enters her
Tastes her…Savors her
Her womanhood is like pink cotton candy melting on my tongue
As I swallow each drop her fingers knead my shoulders…[need my shoulders]
Instantly our bodies are entangled
She on top of me
Me beneath her
Legs spread welcoming her
She enters me…deeply

Finding places, I buried…places I never knew existed
Underneath the moonlight, we are unable to tell where her body ends and mine
begins
We have become one
Connected through our contours and curves…

Babygirl, I love you.
All of you.
Especially all the wet, sticky parts.

COULD THIS BE?

Could this be love?
Is it too soon?
Does the Universe condemn a rose for blooming out of season
Or does it just accept that sometimes things just are
Just because they are?

Some things cannot be explained…

Love cannot be contained by time…

I didn't enter into her gates wanting to fall in love
It was the furthest thing from my mind
But the moment I saw her smile I fell in love
With the woman that I knew she was
I fell in love with the woman that she inspired me to be

I fell in love with the thought of a possibility
That perhaps…just perhaps…

This could be love

THERE IS NOTHING SEXIER THAN WHEN SHE ARCHES HER BACK,
CUMS IN MY MOUTH AND MOANS, "GOOD GIRL."

SHE SMELLS LIKE...

She smells like home
Like warm sunshine and summer breezes
She smells like comfort & peace
Like lazy Sunday afternoons
She smells like freshly made pineapple juice on ice

She smells like destiny & possibilities

She smells like
making love & soft moans
Like naughty words whispered
on shallow breaths
She smells like candlewax dripped
over bodies glistening in sweat
She smells like intimacy and passion

She smells like joy and happiness
Like understanding
She smells like fire
Like morning dew and raindrops
She smells like stargazer lilies
Like ocean waves
She smells like warmth and gentleness

She smells like...love

UNAFRAID

I didn't know how to tell her that I was afraid of loving her
That my life only allowed for people to get so close
Before I sabotaged my own happiness
How did I begin to tell her that I was fearful that our laughter would be one of
those memories I recalled as love songs played over speakers in a smoke-filled
dive bar
How did I begin to tell her that I longed to love her the way that she deserved
to be loved
Uninhibited & Unrestrained
But I was too afraid of being hurt, of being rejected
Memories of a broken childhood clouded my senses
Our love didn't make sense
The way we laughed didn't make sense
The way we made love didn't make sense
Nothing about us made sense
But it worked, we worked
We understand each other
It still escapes my reasoning how can she understand me when at times I don't
even understand myself
My brokenness didn't scare her off…didn't make her run away
I believe that is the part that made me even more afraid
How did I begin to accept that she accepted me
All of me…not the idea of me
She loved me simply because I am
And my I am was enough
And that frightened me
For once I was enough
So I wanted to love her freely, recklessly, with abandon
Just once I wanted to experience what it was like to just love and to be loved
I understood that loving that freely was a choice
So I made mine
To love her unafraid even while I was afraid
To accept her for who she is
To care for her when she is hurting
To stand alongside her when she needed me
To hold her hand when she needs assurance
To support her dreams
I made a choice to stop hiding and to start loving…her
Realizing that loving in the face of fear is revolutionary…

REVOLUTION

Revolution
/ ˌrev·ə'lu·ʃən/

a sudden and great change, esp. the violent change of
a system of government:
the overthrow of a government by those who are governed
a sudden, often violent uprising from the people to change the political
system

FORMATION

Formation
Said firmly with no hesitation
Concern for yo tears recently went on vacation
We are unbothered by your hatin' and condemnation
It's simply confirmation
And the very reason we're celebratin'
This is the manifestation of a bloodline that birthed a nation
We ain't offspring, we're the foundation of creation
When you sip from Mother Earth you're drinkin' our libations
This is lyrical liberation
You wanna be mad at something? Be mad at the blood on the hands of this
nation
This is the reincarnation of a spirit that has no expiration
This is old Negro Spiritual Salvation
That down South church fan wavin' congregation
This is Bey's black fist standing on Roc Nation
But since you seem to need clarification
This is for 40 acres and a mule reparations
Picking cotton in fields with no compensation
For not telling slaves about emancipation
For Rosa being told to get in the back of yo' transportation
For Sara Baartman's humiliation at the hands of your exploitation
For co-opting a culture with weak imitations
For Martin and Malcom's assassinations
For countless years of segregation
For every time you told our sistas & brothas to assume the formation
For keeping them in a system chained to probation
For a racist system masquerading as fair administration
For Sandra Bland dead on the floor of a police station
For smallpox infestation
This is for Tuskegee experimentation
For telling us why All Lives Matter with no qualifications
This is for brutally raping a nation
For Eric Garner's suffocation
This is for a black male shot dead at Fruitvale Station
And this voice, this voice is the reincarnation of every one you murdered with
no justification
Now YOU bow down….and simply assume the formation!

SPACES

It is difficult to stand in spaces
Spaces that were not designed for me
Spaces that were not constructed for people that look like me
Spaces that scream, "You do not belong here!"
Spaces that feel like sandpaper against my blackness

Coarse…Rough…Painful…Uneasy

Spaces that are void of signs but still I can see them hanging in a not so distant memory
Signs that separated water fountains and restaurants
Blatantly reminding people that these spaces were not made for them
And although the signs no longer remain the architecture and atmosphere is constructed in such a way
That I know and we know that these are not our spaces
We are simply standing in borrowed time to entertain the master's masses

It is difficult to stand in these spaces and be me, fully me
Code switching my vernacular to make you feel comfortable
Why does my life have to dress itself in discomfort for you be at ease?
Why does my gender make you uncomfortable in these spaces?
Why does my skin feel so heavy in these spaces?
Why does my hair have to look a certain way to stand in these spaces?

These are spaces that I no longer want to reside in
I don't enjoy these spaces
I no longer desire to subject myself to these spaces
But then I am reminded, as I stand in these spaces
And I see the faces of 2 little black girls watching me perform in awe because I am a person with kinky hair like them and skin that looks like theirs and lips that look like theirs, standing in these spaces
Spaces that have been designed in ways that have spoken to them at an early age, reminding them that, "Some spaces just ain't for your kind."

You see that is why I stand in these spaces, being a shout in these spaces

For every Black person that surveyed a room to see if there was anyone that looked like them in these spaces
For every woman that stood at the head of a boardroom table wondering if she was equal in these spaces

For every LGBTQ person that wondered if they could safely be themselves in
these spaces
For every Muslim woman that wondered can I wear my hijab in these spaces

I remember those that stood in spaces not designated for them

That marched on roads not paved for them
That sat in seats on buses not earmarked them
That sat down at counters and endured the humiliation of sitting in spaces not
designed for them
So that one day I too could stand in these spaces

That is why I am in these spaces! Standing boldly in these spaces!

It is for every one that came before me that sat in spaces that made them ill at
ease
That sipped water at the colored only fountain
That marched into integrated schools and knew they were one of nine
It is for every Black performer that stood on stages so that one day little Black
kids could know that they too could stand on these stages
It is for my mother, my mother, that stood in the space of a cotton field picking
cotton for eighty cents a day

See, that is why I am in these spaces

It is for every one that will come after me
For everyone to know they have a right to be in these spaces, to have seat at the
table in these spaces, to have a voice in these spaces, to have influence in these
spaces
That is why I stand in spaces that make me uncomfortable
Speaking boldly against injustice even now while some of you sit looking at me
and now you feel uncomfortable

But today you have heard me
You cannot unsee me!

In this space, I belong...In this space...this space
We are here & We belong here! In this space!

WE ARE NOT RAGDOLLS

We are not ragdolls
To be flung across classrooms
Jail cells
Highway streets
And sidewalks
We are not ragdolls
To be tossed about haphazardly
Stomped on
Tased
Guns held to temples
With hatred spewing from lips falsely painted with so-called authority
We are not ragdolls
Our names are not Raggedy Ann
Wide-eyed dolls with red yarn hair
Sitting on shelves until you feel like playing with us
And painted on lips that don't ask questions
We have voices
Voices that buck the system
Yet we are STILL women
With skin that bruises
Bones that break
We bleed
We ache
We hurt
And yes we heal
But something is forever altered
When someone steps into your being
And pumps fists against your femininity
And everything that you ever knew about being a woman
With each hit
Each name
Is changed
Because you never saw a woman
In all her splendor
In all her glory
In her magnificence
In your plantation flashbacks
You saw black
And for you
That was raggedy

And she was no longer a human being
But that black thing you can fling
Across classrooms
In front of black men
That sadly sat in position
Instead of defending this woman
She was not a ragdoll
Her name is not Raggedy Ann
She has a name
She is a woman
That breaks
That hurts
That bleeds
Just like me
And we are not ragdolls

STRANGE FRUIT 2

Southern trees bear strange fruit
Blood on the leaves and blood at the root
Black bodies swinging in the southern breeze
Strange fruit hanging from the poplar trees

Mike Brown was just 18 years old when he was killed in Ferguson, Missouri by a police officer on August 9, 2014. His body lay in the street for just over 4 hours as the world watched another Black man be murdered for daring to be Black.

Pastoral scene of the gallant south
The bulging eyes and the twisted mouth
Scent of magnolias, sweet and fresh
Then the sudden smell of burning flesh

His death was one that ignited a movement.

Here is fruit for the crows to pluck
For the rain to gather, for the wind to suck
For the sun to rot, for the trees to drop
Here is a strange and bitter crop

2 Songwriters: Lewis Allan / Maurice Pearl / Dwayne P Wiggins
Strange Fruit lyrics © Warner/Chappell Music, Inc

SOMETHING ABOUT THE RAIN

CNN news reporter, Don Lemon interviewed the mothers of Mike Brown, Trayvon Martin and Sean Bell; Lesley McSpadden, Sybrina Fulton and Valerie Bell (respectively).

Each of the mother's sons were murdered by the police. During the interview Lemon asked, "Do you go around the house, in the kitchen, do you talk to Trayvon?" Both Valerie Bell and Sybrina Fulton said, "Yes."

Lemon then asked Mike Brown's mother, "Do you do the same thing, Lesley?"

She replied, "Especially when it rains. Yep."

"When it rains, why?" Lemon asked.

"Something about the rain. Something about it."

"That makes you want to…" Lemon started and Lesley replied, "I feel him. He's there."

This poem is dedicated to all the mothers who sit looking out the window counting the raindrops.

AIN'T I A MOTHER?

There isn't a day that goes by that I don't think of him
Especially when the rain falls
He loved the rain
Said God was making everything new
I wonder if he's there
In the clouds
In the dew
Does he hear me?
Can he see me?
Sometimes I hear his voice on the wind
See his smile in the face of a child
Fragments of him scattered in memories

I'm clutching for anything to make sense
Who picks up the pieces of a soul that has been shattered?
Will I ever feel whole again?
I just want to feel…normal
They said this would get easier
That time would soothe the pain
Yet life hasn't given me a moment to grieve
And Ain't I A Mother?
Ain't I got a right to hurt?
He was my only child
Ain't I got a right to cry?
Ain't I got a right to weep for grandchildren that I will never know?
Ain't I got a right to my sorrow?

My son was a good kid
But good Black boys scream from the grave daily
And every day I hear him
Wailing among the willows
As I watch the sun set just beneath the horizon
I listen
Hoping for new day that never seems to come
You didn't see him.
You never saw him
His beauty
His heart
His compassion

How many shots did it take?

What were his last words?
Was anyone there to hold his hand?
Was he cold?
How long did it take him to die?
Did he ask for me?
You see I was always there to ease his pain
Bandage his wounds, tell him that he was gonna be okay
But this time… it won't be…okay
I promised I would protect him
I would cover him
And now you want me to understand
When you say that you are sorry?

Did you notice that his blood was red like yours?
That his heart beat like yours
That he had dreams like your little boy
I told him he would pushed beyond barriers…
I told him he would carry the weight of the world in his hands
I long to rewind time
See him again
Tell him this world will be a better place
Tell him this world says its sorry
Tell him that one day his skin won't be his sentence
Tell him that one day he will soar
That one day he will chase the stars
That he would change the world
That one day this world will embrace him
That one day…he will stretch his arms and fly
Tell him that one day this world will let him just be
But rewinding time is gone
My life is nothing now but grasping for second chances

Where do I go from here?
Where do we go from here?
When are we going to pull back the mask?
When are we going to face the truth?
When will we start to talk with each other
My son didn't die so that we would be quiet
People don't die so that we can be whispers
I declare that we will not be silenced any longer
We will no longer be invisible
I hear you son and I vow to be your shout among crowds of whispers
My son's death will not be in vain

I am the voice of our ancestors, of generations
I am the voice of old Negro spirituals
I am the shoulders that carry the weight of suffering
I am the heart of a mother
So no longer do I wait…
No longer do we wait…
Today
We speak
We shout
We yell
Vowing that the blood that wails, crying out, rustling through the wind will be heard…

YOU WERE BORN TO BE A PROBLEM

In the Souls of Black Folk W.E.B. Du Bois eloquently penned, "Between me
and the other world there is ever an unasked question: unasked by some
through feelings of delicacy; by others through the difficulty of rightly framing
it. All, nevertheless, flutter round it, "How does it feel to be a problem?"
How does it feel not to just have a problem… but to be the problem?
That your very existence, the fact you are breathing air is problematic?
How does it feel to be a problem?
The usual suspect, murdered live on social media by those sworn to serve and
protect, gunned down in the streets holding Skittles and tea, memorialized on
Twitter with Rest in Peace shirts and hashtags all while they continue to fill out
toetags?
How does it feel knowing that 32% of Black males live in poverty?
How does it feel to know that Black and Brown boys get expelled faster than
any other race?
How does it feel to scream at the top of your lungs and no one hears you?
How does it feel to be a problem?
A problem is often seen as something negative, unwelcomed, harmful and
needing to be "dealt with"
A problem can also be defined as an unexpected disruption in a system
So, my answer to the question, "How does it feel to be a problem?"
IS THAT YOU WERE BORN TO BE A PROBLEM!
You were not created to just go along to get along
The blood that flows through your veins is the same blood that beat through
the hearts of men and women that were a problem
People that were born to disrupt the system, that challenged the status quo
People that dared to believe that this world could be different
Toussaint Louverture was a problem
Frederick Douglas was a problem
Harriet Tubman was a problem
Nat Turner was a problem
Jackie Robinson was a problem
Fannie Lou Hamer was a problem
Martin Luther King was a problem
Ida B. Wells was a problem
Marcus Garvey was a problem
Lucy Parsons was a problem
Fred Hampton was a problem
Malcom X was a problem
Assata Shakur was a problem
Barack Obama was a problem

Trayvon Martin, Sandra Bland and Mike Brown were problems that shook a
sleeping nation to a movement
You were born to be a problem!
You were created to disrupt the system
You are here to challenge the status quo
You are designed to question those in authority, to ask the hard questions
Why are you afraid of my Blackness?
Why is my wallet always seen as a gun?
Why is it okay to take healthcare away from those that might need it the most?
Why are we abusing people that want to protect the right to have clean water?
Why do women still get paid less than men for doing the same job?
Why do 62 people hold as much wealth as the poorest 3.5 billion people in the
world?
Why does my zip code determine my life expectancy?
Why do you incarcerate more Black and Brown males than any other race?
Why does the educational system expel us at an alarming rate?
Why is the drug epidemic now a health crisis when years ago, no one cared
when crack was ravaging the Black community?
Why can't I shop or eat a balanced meal in my own neighborhood?
Why do you turn your backs on the very people whose backs you walked on to
build a nation?
Why does my existence threaten you?
Your job is to ask why?!
You were born to be a problem!
Because you were born with possibility, power, promise and potential
You were created to confront injustice
To be a thorn in the side of inequality!
You were made to be a voice for the voiceless
You see, you be that glitch in the Matrix!
If you were not a problem
They wouldn't be after you so hard
If you were not a problem
They wouldn't create laws to hold you back
If you were not a problem
They wouldn't try to squash your dreams
If you were not a problem
They wouldn't try to beat you down!
If you were not a problem
They wouldn't care about you organizing
If you were not a problem
They wouldn't infiltrate your community with drugs and alcohol
If you were not a problem
They wouldn't care that you stand up in your community

The reason they are after you is because they see your power
Because Strength always overpowers weakness
Light always outshines darkness
Like Thomas Merton said, "How do I begin to tell you that you are all walking
around shining like the sun?"
So, when they ask you, "How does it feel to be a problem?"
Stand proud, stand strong, stand in your authority and declare,
"It feels amazing because I was born to be a problem!"

EVERYBODY WANTS TO BE BLACK
UNTIL IT'S TIME TO BE BLACK

Everybody wants to be Black until it's time to be Black
I said everybody wants to be Black until it's time to be Black
Being Black is more than just a feeling
It's more than pickin' us apart and takin' what you find appealing
You put on Black like a costume
Wear darker shades of foundation to capture our hues
See everyone wants our rhythm but don't want nothin' to do with our blues
You want our music, food and our soul
Someone tell me how in the hell do you whitewash cornrows?
We codeswitch to survive while ya'll stay stealing our slang
God help me if I hear another White person say fleek,
tea or shade
You sprinkle Black on your bland life like it's seasoning
Call appropriation, appreciation as if that's good reasoning
Circling around Black content like a vulture
Steal everything that's Black pawnin' it off as your culture
Everything we do is co-opted
If we invented it rest assured a White person copped it
From our skin, lips, to the roundness of our backsides
White repackaged Black and turned it into a franchise
The way ya'll steal from us should be criminal
Lackluster, watered-down versions of the original
Everything we do is imitated
But you are sadly mistaken if you think Black can be duplicated
Our excellence can never be replicated
That's the number one reason we are so hated
When you hold us up against each other something is amiss
You see, one is real, the other is counterfeit
This is Black and you can't fake this
Being Black is not something you "put on" it lives within your soul
This ain't store bought, baby this is all natural
This is the real deal and there is no substitute for that
This is love and struggle, joy and pain...This is BLACK.

ALL YOU HAD TO DO WAS PLAY THE GAME, BOY[3]

All you had to do was throw the ball, boy. We concealed this auction block well, didn't we, boy? You didn't know you were on sale, boy? Didn't we tell you to just run, boy? Entertain us, boy. Win championships for us, boy. Stay in your place, boy. Don't you dare get these other , Black men riled up, boy. Didn't we pay you enough, boy? Why can't you just be satisfied, boy? Stand up and salute this flag, boy. Honor your allegiance to the system, boy. Didn't we give you enough money to entice you, boy? How dare you reject your master, boy. Didn't you like your name in lights, boy? Didn't we stroke your ego, boy? All you needed to do was play the game, boy. Keep dancing for us on Monday Night, boy. Make us rich, boy. We don't care if you get hurt, boy. Our job is to break bucks like you, boy. Didn't you know boys like you come a dime a dozen, boy? We can replace you with no thought, boy. Make sure our new boy is a controlled boy. Thought you knew we don't trust Negroes to be the quarterback anyways, boy. We did you a favor, boy. How dare you turn your back on us, boy. If you are kneeling, it will be before us, boy. Ain't this game your God, boy? Don't you see how everyone else bows down before us, boy? Don't you know what we do to Negroes like you, boy? Back in the day, we let Negroes like you sway from the trees, boy. Make an example outta you, so other Negroes will stay in their place, boy. Don't you smell that strange fruit in the air, boy? All you had to do was just shut up, boy. We don't have to kill you, boy. All we have to do is silence you, boy.

The NFL is comprised of 70% African American males. Black Men have the power to dismantle an industry.

There is a story I once heard, could be fact, fiction or part fact and part fiction, however the sentiment of the story is something I will never forget. One day a man was walking through the circus passing the elephants, and he wondered how such a powerful, gigantic creature could be held in place with just a rope and a stake in the ground. The elephant's freedom was just on the other side of believing that it could break the rope. When the man saw the trainer he asked him, "Why doesn't the elephant just break the rope and leave this place of bondage and return to his home where he will find sustenance and freedom in his original habitat where he will thrive?"

The trainer smiled and said, "When the elephant is very young and small, we tie a rope to his leg, and it's enough to hold the elephant in place. No matter how the elephant might struggle, he cannot break loose. As the elephant grows older,

---

3 Video All You Had To Do Was Play the Game Boy
https://www.youtube.com/watch?v=OjiuvLzhCrI&feature=youtu.be

he has been conditioned over time to believe that he cannot break the rope so, in turn, the elephant never tries to get free."

Freedom is often connected to the ability to recognize that there is no rope that can hold you. Once you decide to walk in your power and authority you can no longer be bound. Restricted freedom is still bondage and it costs. You may not pay now, but the bill always comes due and the oppressor will always want to collect payment.

One voice can be a spark. United voices can ignite a movement. One voice can bring awareness to a system. A multitude of voices can dismantle it.

My brothers in the NFL, you are no longer enslaved. You have all the power. You hold all the cards. You have the power collectively to stand for someone that knelt for our brothers and sisters that were murdered with no regard. As Assata said, "It is our duty to fight for our freedom. It is our duty to win. We must love each other and support each other. We have nothing to lose but our chains."

You have nothing to lose but your chains...

MASTER'S SHADOW

In typical fashion
Still
You have master at my back

Even in this gesture, he and I stand on opposite sides

Was I not enough?
Did I not do enough?
Did I not risk enough?
Did I not free enough
To stand alone
On a piece of paper
That only has value
Because you deem it has value?

It is almost ironic
My face seems similar to 3/5's of paper…

If you are going to give us freedom…give us freedom
If you are going to celebrate women…celebrate a woman
If you are going to embrace Black…embrace it wholeheartedly
With no fear of (back)(lash)

When we are truly free
Truly liberated
My legacy
Will be seen coming and going
With no remnants of master in the shadows

WHO PROTECTS BLACK WOMEN?

Why you want to fly Blackbird₄
You ain't ever gonna fly
Why you want to fly Blackbird
You ain't ever gonna fly
No place big enough for holding all the tears you're gonna cry

"I know what it like to wanna sing…and have it beat outch'ya." This line was spoken in The Color Purple by the character Miss Sophia played brilliantly by Oprah Winfrey. Miss Sophia was asked by a White woman named Miss Millie if she wanted to be her maid and Miss Sophia replied, "Hell no." That reply was enough for a White man to step in and assault Miss Sophia. What resulted afterward was a vicious attack that not only broke Miss Sophia's body but also broke her spirit. What was once a robust, outspoken woman returned home from spending years in jail, subjected to being Miss Millie's maid, quiet and shattered. It was not until the lead character Ms. Celie stands up against her abusive husband that we catch a glimpse of the former Miss Sophia.

This scene is one that came to my mind after witnessing a White man named Daniel Taylor** assault Yasmine James, a Black woman that was taking his order at McDonald's. Taylor can be seen in the video lunging at Yasmine in what appears to be an attempt to drag her over the counter. In what I assume was, fearing for her safety, James defends herself, hitting Taylor until he releases her, while many of her co-workers simply look on. You would think after watching this man assault Yasmine James, he would immediately be put out of the store. However, that did not happen. From the video, it appears the manager is still trying to serve Taylor. And in fact, Taylor goes on to say, "I want her ass fired right now," as if he has done nothing wrong.

Yasmine yells back to him, "No, you're finna go to jail. You put your hands on me first!"

Taylor responded, "I couldn't control you. I was just asking you a question, bitch!"

And there we have it. "I couldn't control you."

---

4 Blackbird Nina Simone Written By: Herbert Sacker, Nina Simone

How dare this Black woman deny him what many have said was a simple issue over a straw. And because he couldn't "control her" to him that warranted assaulting her. And still, even that was not enough. It was not until Taylor kicked another female employee in the stomach that he was asked to leave the McDonald's. Why wasn't he asked to leave when he assaulted Yasmine? Was she not enough? How many times would he have to hit Yasmine for it to be enough?

'Cause your mama's name was lonely
And your daddy's name was pain
And they call you little sorrow
'Cause you'll never love again
So why you want to fly Blackbird
You ain't ever gonna fly

Who defends the Black woman? Who speaks out for the Black woman? Who shouts for the Black woman? Who cares about the Black woman? Who says Me Too for the Black woman? Who protects the Black woman?

Over and over again, we have watched countless videos of Black women and girls being assaulted. We have watched Black girls on the ground with the knee of a White man in their backs. We have watched a Black girl thrown across the classroom like a rag doll. We have watched a Black woman assaulted on the floor of WaffleHouse. We have watched our little Black girls murdered with no regard. We have watched a Black woman punched over and over again on the side of a highway. We have witnessed Black women murdered by their lovers. The hashtags of Black women murdered by the police are endless. The names and numbers of Black women and girls that have been raped are astronomical. And this world keeps turning. It never pauses to understand when a Black woman screams for help the earth is trembling.

Who hears us?

Who is weeping for us?

Who is standing with us?

Who shares our stories?

When will our issues be front page news?

When will we stop being props for your election campaigns and marches?

You ain't got no one to hold you
You ain't got no one to care

If you'd only understand dear
Nobody wants you anywhere
So why you want to fly Blackbird
You ain't ever gonna fly

This world demands EVERYTHING from Black women and offers Black women NOTHING in return. And we are tired. We have given everything we can and then some. We have paid debts that we didn't incur with our very lives. We have upheld our end of a bargain that was NEVER for us. We keep waiting and wondering when this world will defend us? When will this world see our value? Are Black women not included in your agenda? Does our plight not sell enough t-shirts and pins and tote bags? Does this incident not fit in with how you define intersectionality? Is the victim not sophisticated enough? Is the victim too Black to fit your agenda? Will she not look good in a pink pussy cat hat? When will you stand up for her and Black women just like her? When will the marches take place for Black women that have been assaulted? When will you shed a tear for Jazmine Barnes, a little Black girl that was murdered? When will this world SEE us? Not just physically see us in an attempt to emulate everything that we are outwardly but when will this nation show us true sawubona- meaning I see you, recognize you, and I connect with your humanity. I understand that I cannot be all that I can be until you are all that you can be. When will that happen? To be honest, I am no longer holding my breath for anyone besides Black women to see me. If you haven't seen us by now, you never will.

But I see you, Black women. I see you in all your glory, wonder and splendor. I see you in your beauty and your gentleness. I see you in your love and your passion and even your pain and sorrow. I see you in your intelligence and wisdom. I see you, and I will protect you. Because I want you to sing, blackbird. I want you to fly, blackbird. Because you deserve to soar.

BY ANY MEANS NECESSARY

Baldwin said, "To be a Negro in America & relatively conscious is to be in a
constant state of rage."
Since ya'll want to treat us like animals then consider me uncaged
Every day I see the sun rise I wake up enraged
Wondering if today will be the day Black America goes on a rampage
And you think you bout that life cause you post a hashtag on your page?
While I'm canning food and storing water, plotting how to live in these last
days
And you have the nerve to ask me why I am angry as if need to give you a
reason
Y'all are the biggest perpetrators of racism, injustice, corruption and treason
Yet somehow you got the world fooled believin' we are the problem
We seek restoration, peace and healing but you continue to be the toxin
This ground that we stand on for Black people ain't never be sovereign
The very nature of America at its fundamental core has always been rotten
Land that was acquired by ill-gotten gains, built on the backs of slaves
You raped the Motherland then have the nerve to say, "Don't make this about
race."
Everything is about race so you need to wake the fuck up!
Got the nerve to tell me I need to be quiet. My rebuttal is shut the fuck up!
How do you expect me to close my mouth?
When Aiyana Stanley Jones was killed just sleeping on her couch
Alton Sterling was killed outside of a store selling CD's
Eric Garner last breath was taken yelling, "I can't breathe!"
Trayvon's life was taken after he bought Skittles and some tea
Terence Crutcher was murdered and they blamed it on PCP
Mike Brown died in the street simply holding up his hands
"I meant to reach for my taser" was the excuse given for Oscar Grant
Failure to signal is what led to the death of Sandra Bland
Playing with a toy gun on a playground led to the death of Tamir Rice
Tashii Brown was murdered under the glow of Vegas lights
Sean Bell was murdered just before he was supposed to be married
Philando died reaching for his wallet stating he had the right to carry
A "rough ride" was the excuse for Freddie Gray
The reason for Rekia Boyd's murder was wrong time and wrong place
Yvette Smith was murdered in just 3 seconds because she opened her front
door
Natasha McKenna died shackled and tasered for 17 minutes on a jailhouse
floor
Walter Scott was shot in the back and murdered running away

Amadou Diallo was shot 41 times and they said they "made a mistake"
Jordan Davis was killed for playing his music too loud
Jordan Edwards was murdered for trying to leave a party crowd
The list of murders at YOUR hands is senseless and endless
And I don't know where to go from here unless we end this
So, when you ask me why I'm angry just take a look at this list
This is why I'm angry and pissed off
And this is why I stand for justice at any cost
And I pray that justice comes quick, swift and in a hurry
Cause at this point I'm ready to get justice by any means necessary…

TEARDROPS & TRUST FUNDS

I saw teardrops and trust funds
White men in suits that could fund dreams
That Maria and Maybelle have long suppressed
Because they learned early in life
That dreams don't pay bills or put food on the table

Rotund bellies
Swollen from years of aged bourbon and cold beer
As they clink glasses together and cheer another day…
Our tears are just salty appetizers
White men dine on choice cut meats a man named Miguel sliced from bovine
That was a blood sacrifice to these (g)ods
They do not know his name
Or that he gets paid under the table
Or that his family lives in cages we built
They don't care
As long as their lives stay uninterrupted by our concerns

They snort arrogance and powdered privilege
Pure and uncut

Liver spotted hands
Hold all the cards
Moving us like chess pieces

They are the masters of a warped universe
They made us build

We punch the clock to our own demise
Drugged up on Paxil
Opioids to mask the pain
Xanax to paint on the smile
Merlot to swallow it all down
Ambien to make us sleep
We drown in the white noise
Trying to drown out the White noise
Longing to forget that tomorrow we will do it again and again and again…
We are cogs in this machine
That feeds them
As they dine on our flesh
We tweet our horror in soundbites

Reliving trauma in Instagramable quotes
Where we pretend we don't feel the pain
From the gnashing of teeth

HANNAH L. DRAKE

WHY ARE YOU ANGRY, WHITE MAN?

Only White men are allowed to be angry…
So I ask…
Why are you angry, White man?
Did the world give you too much?
Did too many women bow down to your needs?
Didn't she swallow just the way you like it?
Didn't the church make you the face of the world's Savior?
Aren't you the only one allowed to be our superheroes?

Why are you angry, White man?
Was the trust fund too big?
Was the silver spoon not polished to your liking?
Didn't Hollywood make you the perpetual movie star?
Didn't we spit shine your Bostonians?
Didn't you enjoy the music from the violin of Nero?
Aren't you warmed by the flames of a nation burning?

Why are you angry, White man?
Aren't the laws written in your favor?
Didn't you write the documents that govern this nation?
Didn't history rewrite itself to make you the benevolent victor?
Hasn't everything always been yours?
Don't you always take whatever you want?
Hasn't the world refused to tell you no?

Why are you angry, White man?
Was private school not good enough?
Did Ivy League not suit your requirements?
Didn't nepotism work in your favor?
Don't you have the shiniest toys?

Why are you angry, White man?
Is it because you can feel us on your heels?
You hear the pounding of an ancestral army chasing after you
The same way you unleashed bloodhounds on them
You may have forgotten
We didn't
We see the panic in your jaundiced eyes
It is not anger you display
It is fear.
As you realize the day of reckoning will soon be upon you.

DO NOT MOVE OFF THE SIDEWALK CHALLENGE:
HOLDING YOUR SPACE IN A WHITE WORLD

Last year, I was in the airport on the rolling walkway with clear directions posted before stepping on the sidewalk to 'stand on the right or walk on the left.' There was a White man in front of me that disregarded the sign and stood in the middle of the rolling walkway preventing anyone from passing him. Behind me, I could hear someone approaching, and I turned around and saw a middle age Black woman walking briskly with her rolling suitcase flying behind her. I pressed myself and my luggage against the side rail to move out of her way and allow her easy access to pass me. She whizzed by me and in front of her was the White man, oblivious that she was behind him and in an apparent rush. He never turned around, never moved and never once thought that others behind him might need to pass. While I would like to say the Black woman, leaped over him, luggage in tow in a single bound, she stopped dead in her tracks. She never said a word. She never politely tapped the man on the shoulder to say, "Excuse me, may I get by you?" She just accepted that he was not going to move and for some reason even though she was in an apparent rush, she made a choice not to ask for him to cede the space for her to pass. She waited for the rolling walkway to come to an end, waited for him to saunter off the walkway then immediately took off in a sprint heading towards her gate. That small interaction stayed with me my entire flight.

As I made my connecting flight, I was looking forward to having pizza at the airport. I cannot recall the name of the restaurant, but it has the best pizza with prosciutto, arugula and cooked eggs on top surrounded by hot, creamy goat cheese. After I got my pizza, I sat down at an empty counter and put my earphones in, anxiously ready to take a huge bite. Before I could get my first bite, a White man walked up to the opposite side of the counter, facing me, with his food. I looked up at him then looked down at the completely empty counter space (besides me sitting at it) wondering why he chose to stand directly in front of me as he added salt to his food? Typically, I would move down, but after witnessing the Black woman on the rolling walkway, I made a decision, "**I am NOT moving! I do not care if he wants to stand there until I have finished every bite of this pizza, I refuse to move to accommodate him!**" After he enjoyed a few bites of his food and noticed that I was not going to move, he packed up his belongings and moved to the end of the counter.

Victory!

It was just that easy. I made a conscious decision as a Black woman to hold my space. I was not going to cede my space to a White person because that is what was expected of me. Now, before you read any further, this is not a blog about being rude, impolite, etc. I believe as an "average" human being we understand that there are sometimes you must and should cede your space. If you are in the way of someone that has some physical challenges or someone is elderly and as a result, has some physical issues that is different. I am not talking about ordinary, everyday courtesy we extend to others for often apparent reasons. That is NOT what I am talking about so please do not message me about that or make this blog about that. If you do, you are taking the easy way out of this blog and not looking at the totality of what I am discussing.

I am talking about Black people, particularly Black women and People of Color being cognizant of how they navigate throughout spaces making accommodations for White people and White people having an expectation that Black people or People of Color must navigate their bodies to allow White people access in spaces. This is more than someone being rude; this is about White people feeling as if Black bodies should accommodate them in spaces and if we do not, it is seen as the Black person being rude, unpleasant and intimidating.
An example of this is a recent incident documented by Frederick T. Joseph, who took a photo of a White woman placing her feet on his dining tray on an airplane. The airline staff did not address the woman and when Joseph asked the woman to move her feet, she accused him of disrupting her flight. According to the article, when the flight staff asked the woman to remove her feet she stated, "If I put one foot down, I want to be accommodated for accommodating him." In this space, the White woman felt she was well within her right to infringe on Joseph's space and when told she could not, she wanted to be accommodated as if respecting his space was doing him a favor.

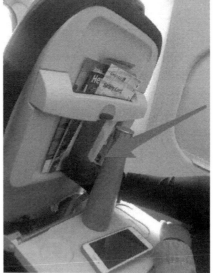

Photo by Frederick T. Joseph/Twitter

Black people and People of Color accommodate spaces for White people so often that we may not even realize that we are doing it or how ingrained it is in Black culture to cede your space. I hadn't given thought to the incident in the airport in a while; however, yesterday I read a Twitter thread by, Tatiana Mac and the memory of that day instantly came to my mind.

While thousands of people shared, understood and could relate to Tatiana's story, there was an exchange by a White woman named Liberty Warrior that brought the thread full circle. (I am providing screenshots below because I knew it would only be a matter of time before Liberty Warrior blocked me and true to form, when I went to the thread today, she had blocked me. Because I deal with women like Liberty Warrior often, I had already taken screen shots of the conversation because I knew she would do that. That is often the modus operandi of people like her. When they do not want to face the truth, they block the truth.)

Even in the virtual arena, Black people and People of Color are expected to cede their space. If you look at the thread, Liberty Warrior was repeatedly asked to remove herself from Tatiana's thread, and she refused. Instead of starting her own thread in her own virtual space, she felt it was necessary to list all the times that People of Color have made her feel inferior in spaces on Tatiana's thread. She could not understand that she was doing the very thing that Tatiana was talking about just in a virtual space. When I mentioned this to her, she called me sweetheart, and when I told her that was not my name, she proceeded to tell me that SHE can call me whatever she wants. Why does she feel that she has that authority? Because in many spaces, even virtual spaces, many White people think that Black people and People of Color must step back, bow down, and relinquish their virtual space to accommodate their racism.

For centuries, White America has dictated how Black people can navigate our own bodies in spaces. It is not just the physical space itself being regulated by White people but the actual way Black people can use their bodies in these spaces. For instance, there was a time in this country that Black people were required to step off the sidewalk if a White person was approaching them and allow the White person to pass, before stepping on the sidewalk again. According to Dr. Ronald L. F. Davis of California State University, Jim Crow laws provided "racial etiquette" for Black people. Black people were required to be "agreeable and non-challenging, even when the White person was mistaken about something."

Black people are often told how much space we are allowed to take up, and our space is often infringed upon to accommodate White people. If we are tall, our height is used as a way to demonize us. This was evident when 12-year-old Tamir Rice was murdered within minutes by the police in Cleveland, Ohio. Tamir was described by now ousted police union president, Steve Loomis as, "Menacing. He's 5-feet-7, 191 pounds. He wasn't that little kid you're seeing in pictures. He's a 12-year-old in an adult body." Tamir could not help his height. Yet his physical appearance was used to justify his murder. If we take up too much space, it is a problem. Black people and People of Color are acutely aware of our bodies in spaces. I have been in meetings, and everyone has been acknowledged, but me or I am acknowledged last. I have sat in spaces, and after a quick introduction, people cease directing any comments to me. It is almost as if I am The Invisible Black Person by the door just taking up space. I am learning after the airport incident, to hold my space. I am here, and I will not apologize if me holding my space disrupts your day.

My challenge for Black people and People of Color, particularly Black women and Women of Color, is to hold your space. I challenge you for the next 24-48 hours to be aware of your body in spaces and do not move for a White person or make any apologies for physically occupying any space. Be mindful of how you navigate sidewalks, who moves to accommodate you and who doesn't. If someone infringes on your space, do you speak up or remain silent? Make a mental note of any time you feel you were "expected" to move and the reaction of the other person when you didn't. Take note of how people accommodate others in spaces. Was it frightening or empowering to hold your space? Do you think people felt you were intimidating? How did you feel at the end of the day?

For White people, I challenge you for the next 24-48 hours to be aware of how to treat Black people and People of Color in spaces. Do you have an expectation that Black people and People of Color should move out of your way? How many times do you insert yourself and your comments into

virtual spaces because you feel it is your right without reading and listening to People of Color that have stated their truth on a particular issue? Do you speak around the Black person as if they are not in the room? Do you interrupt People of Color when they are speaking? Are you cutting a Black person or a Person of Color in line because you feel that is your right? Also be aware of how it feels to be cognizant of how your body navigates spaces and imagine how that would feel to do that at the very least for 8 hours out of each day.

When I held my space at the airport, I felt empowered. I was angry that someone stood right in front of me and started eating as if I was not right there. **I am here. I have every right to be here. I have the right to be in spaces. I will no longer apologize for taking up space nor will I cede my space to a White person simply because that is some unwritten but expected rule. Over the next two days, walk in your authority. Walk as if you want the world to know, "I am here!"** Because you are. And you deserve to be.

WORKING 9-5 IN WHITE SPACES

As a Black woman, I had the unique experience of my first "real" job being at an entirely African-American institution, Bates Memorial Baptist Church. Everyone on staff or in a position of leadership was Black. Not only was everyone Black, for the most part, most of us had some form of post-secondary education from doctorates to bachelor degrees, and we were all united by our love for God, our love for Black people and justice. I remember feeling like my soul was being ripped from my body when the George Zimmerman verdict came in, and the first person I texted was my Pastor, and we expressed our hurt and anger. I didn't have to return to work the next day and pretend the verdict didn't hurt, all of us were angry and we discussed it amongst ourselves as did our daily tasks. Then the death of Mike Brown and many others happened, and across the nation, churches were expressing their solidarity for an end to police brutality. I remember I was going to get a black hoodie made with Black Lives Matter on the front and as I headed out of the doors of the church, I asked Pastor Williams if he would like one and he said, "Of course." His hoodie was adorned with the words, 'I Can't Breathe,' the last words uttered by Eric Garner who was held in a chokehold by NYPD and killed. There was unity amongst us as we all stood for one goal, justice for Black people. I didn't have to go to work and debate my position. I didn't have to listen to someone tell me, "If they would have just complied." I didn't have to hear any stories about White people feeling justified in "standing their ground." I didn't have to hide my pain. I was able to work through the painful experiences with others that understood me as we worked our 9-5 jobs.

Bates Memorial Baptist Church, Dr. F. Bruce Williams, Pastor

Even beyond our solidarity when a tragedy happened in the Black community, there was just understanding for who we are as Black people. I could come to work in my African attire, and no one asked me any silly questions. If there was a day that I wasn't able to finish my braids and had to wear a headwrap to the office, it didn't spark curiosity. There were no negative comments when I shaved all my hair off and wore my afro. No one begged to touch my hair or pet me. If I woke up one morning and wanted to wear my "Descendant of a Field Negro" shirt to work, there were no side-eyes; no one was running to the Human Resources department talking about how they were offended by my t-shirt.

And the food. My goodness, the food! In the church there was an industrial kitchen and boy did we use it! We would bring in collard greens and mac and cheese. We made fried potatoes, cabbage and fried gizzards dripping in hot sauce. And no one asked, "What's that?" No one said, "That smells funny." We would sit in the back room on our lunch break and laugh and slap high fives. We didn't need to codeswitch. We would drop all the g's from the ending of our words, toss in a couple of be's and throw around our slang as we discussed our lives, our hopes, and our dreams.

There were images of Black people on the walls celebrating our history. Every February we made sure to highlight our achievements, but it went beyond just February, 365 days out of the year we were Black, and we embraced that. It was nice to work in a space where I didn't have to think about my skin color. In that space, I was allowed just to be Black even while I was doing my job. I didn't have to leave a part of me at home. I could bring all of my Blackness into the workplace with me with no shame or apologies needed.

Then I left that job and entered into the world of White Spaces. I suddenly found myself in meetings where I was the only Black person. I noticed that many times after an initial introduction comments ceased coming in my direction. I sat in meetings quietly observing. It is funny the things people will say when they have overlooked that you are even in the room. I became hyper-aware of my clothing and folded my Afrocentric t-shirts up and put them in a drawer resolving to wear them on the weekend. I was aware of my language and reserved my slang for my friends and family. Codeswitching just became the norm. I remember once I spoke about taking out my braids and wearing my natural hair, someone commented, "Oh no, Hannah. You have to have your long hair." (Why? Why couldn't I just have my afro?) I was overly aware of the food I brought into the office not wanting food that was part of my heritage and identity to be perceived as having a foul odor.

Most importantly, I became hyper-aware of my skin; it felt so heavy in some of these spaces. I disliked the frivolous small talk of discussing my weekend with people that I didn't know and more than likely had no real interest in how I spent my weekend. While they spoke of weekends filled with hiking and hanging out with friends eating tapas and sipping wine, how did I begin to explain to them I spent my weekend writing or speaking about injustice? That I had just witnessed yet another murder from a police body camera. That I watched the funeral of Stephon Clark and spent an hour crying asking God why? That I found myself a weeping mess on an airplane ride home from a conference after watching the Kalief Browder story asking God, "Why is it so hard to be Black in this world? Why can't people just let us be?" I am certain those are not the answers they want to hear when I am asked about my weekend or what I have been up to lately so instead of saying that I simply say, "It was fine."

Always pretending. Codeswitching was now my life.

Every day I came home exhausted. I would sit in my car outside of my house mindlessly thumbing through my Twitter feed or Facebook. I needed just a moment to breathe. After years of this finally, it dawned on me, Hannah you are exhausted when you come home because all day you have focused not just on your work but also working to be someone that you are not. You are like an animal that has been taken out of its natural habitat and placed in unfamiliar territory which is why you feel anxious all the time. I realized it was a never-ending cycle and it started before work, through work and didn't end until I came home. The time I arrived home was time for me to recover only to wake up and do the same thing the next day and the next day and the next day. And it was exhausting. As I thought about this, I remembered a scene from the X-Men movie series, First Class. Erik Lehnsherr who played a young Magneto, a character that is able to control metal, was speaking with Jennifer Lawrence's character, Raven (Mystique). Raven is able to shapeshift, and her character is typically all blue with piercing yellow eyes. However, to fit into society, she projects herself to look like Jennifer Lawrence. One day she is in the room lifting weights, and Magneto says to her, "If you're using half your concentration to look normal, then you're only half paying attention to whatever else you are doing." While just a movie, those words always stayed with me. I thought about them even more once I returned from Dakar, Senegal. In Dakar, my friend and I were shopping for earrings.

Jennifer Lawrence as Raven (Mystique)

I remember both of us were holding the earrings in such a way that the shop owner would not think we were going to steal them. When we went to pay for the earrings, we realized the shop owner was outside of the store talking to someone. Finally, it dawned on us, in Dakar, our skin color alone was not criminal. There we were free just to show up as our authentic selves. We could shop and not think about someone thinking we were stealing simply because we were Black. There we were free just to be. I had never experienced that before. It was as if the entire world opened up to me and said. "Welcome, Hannah. We've been waiting for you." I could see, and taste and touch and dance and laugh and experience life 100% as a Black woman. I held that moment close to my chest because I knew it would be gone from me soon. I knew I would be back in America where I would have to offer an explanation for my mere existence. Where I was reminded of my Blackness not just daily but hourly.

These reminders came swiftly, and as I thought about writing this blog, two stories came across my social media feed that reminded me of how challenging it is as a Black person to work 9-5 in White spaces. CBS12 reporter AJ Walker had to fight to wear her hair in braids. When she finally was allowed to wear her braids, it was hailed as a victory. Walker stated, "Not many people realize that African-American and other women feel and often are forced to wear hairstyles that the company or news station deems acceptable. The freedom to wear my hair in a style that is part of my culture and a skill handed down to me from my mom gives me a stronger sense of self-esteem, self-worth, and confidence as a person and as a woman." This issue also impacted 17-year-old Kerion Washington as he was denied a job at Six Flags over Texas because of his locs. Can you imagine fighting just to wear your hair a certain way at work? Can you imagine being told the hair that grows out of your head is seen as too extreme for employment?

What if this world was a place where Black people like AJ Walker and Kerion Washington, could show up to work and just be who they are and that was okay? What if the workplace didn't tell us our blackness was unacceptable? I wondered how my life would be if I could show up in the workplace and meetings as just Hannah? While the people I work with now accept me as who I am, I still find myself in many spaces where I am the only or one of few Black people. And while they may love me, there are still unwritten rules about how Black people must navigate White Spaces from 9-5 (and beyond). I often wonder how much more could I accomplish if I could show up 100% me? How much more could I achieve if like the X-Men character Raven I was not spending half my concentration trying to fit into a society that has told me how to speak, how to wear my hair, how to dress, etc. Who could I really be and what could I create if I was allowed just to be me?

For the Black people and People of Color reading this blog, if you would like, please share your experiences working 9-5 in White Spaces. How has this impacted your daily life? What are some of the challenges that you have faced in the workplace? Do you feel the stress of working 9-5 in White spaces and how does that impact your life once you are home?

To the White people reading this blog, have you ever considered how it feels for a Black person or a Person of Color to work in an environment where they never fully show up to work as themselves? Can you imagine going to work and being someone else at a minimum of 8 hours a day your entire working career? Can you see times where you have contributed to a Black person or Person of Color feeling as if they did not belong in the workplace?

I was in Dakar for 2 weeks. That is 20160 minutes. I had 20160 minutes to be free. And for each of those moments I was alive. I long to live in a world where my freedom to be Black isn't regulated to me in minutes. I do not want to show up to work leaving half of me at home. Allow me to show up fully as I am and be amazed at just how authentic and brilliant 100% Black can be.

NANA
FOR CLEANNA, LOVE AUNT NANA

Her laughter reminds me of Ella singing of Summertime
And her heartbeat reminds me of Miles and Coltrane...when the living was easy
Her smile is like kaleidoscopes that drift into prisms of sunlight and rainbows
Her kisses are like butterflies doing pirouettes along my cheek
And although I am not certain, something tells me her hugs is what heaven must feel like
She is 3, she is my niece, and with her lisp, h's were robbed from her tongue so instead of Hannah she awkwardly calls me Nana and I love it
I love everything about her and I even love the 212 times she asks me, "Why, Nana?"
Why do caterpillars slink, why do birds fly why can't I catch clouds in mason jars?
I smile, amazed at her wonder at discovering this world

Right now she still believes that we can
Slide down rainbows into pots of gold
Hitch a ride on Helios's chariot
Laughing as we grasp sunbeams in our hands
She believes that we can long jump with the cows over the moon
Until we tire from gallivanting through the galaxy
Resting our heads on pillows of promise and possibility
Covering ourselves in blankets of a midnight sky
Sleeping on a king size mattress of dreams…

I wish I could take all the innocent parts of her and seal them in a time capsule
Keep her heart locked behind a glass case that says only break when this world is a better place
Wrap her innocence in a cocoon, halt metamorphosis
Before Life steps in, knocking impatiently at the door
You see right now she doesn't see color, she doesn't understand prejudice, she doesn't know what hate feels like, she hasn't tasted the bitter fruit of injustice, she doesn't go to bed hungry, no one has told her what she can't accomplish because she is a girl, no one has told her she is too fat, too loud, too much of everything, Life has not robbed her yet
I cry for what I know is coming down the pike
I look around this world and I weep,

I look into her eyes and I know that we still have a long way to go

We are not finished
How can WE be finished
When 1 billion children worldwide are living in poverty
How can WE be finished
When a gun that was used in the death of a young black man is auctioned off
for thousands of dollars.
How can WE be finished
When 20 children, no older than 7 are murdered in a classroom
How can WE be finished
When a 12-year-old boy is shot to death on a playground in less than 60
seconds
How can WE be finished
When more than half a million people in the US are homeless
How can WE be finished
When 44 million people don't have healthcare and we are debating if it's the
right thing to do
How can WE be finished
When it's STILL a crime to be driving while Black? When we have to start
petitions to remind the world that her life matters.
How can WE be finished
When 9 people are murdered in the pews of a church
No…we are not finished

When I look into the face of my niece, big pools of brown eyes staring back at
me I know that we owe her and ourselves the opportunity to make this world a
better place
Even in all of the pain I still have hope
Even in all of this chaos I still believe that there is goodness in this world
That right now we have an opportunity to live in a different world
A world brimming and vibrant with the vitality of promise
What is the essence of life?, Aristotle asked. To serve others and to do good.
So I will not lose hope
As Martin said, "If you lose hope, somehow you lose the vitality that keeps life
moving, you lose the courage to be, that quality that helps you go on in spite of
it."
So every day I remember his dream

"This will be the day when we bring into full realization the American dream --
a dream yet unfulfilled. A dream of equality of opportunity, of privilege and
property widely distributed; a dream of a land where men will not take
necessities from the many to give luxuries to the few; a dream of a land where
men will not argue that the color of a man's skin determines the content of his
character; a dream of a nation where all our gifts and resources are held not for

ourselves alone, but as instruments of service for the rest of humanity; the dream of a country where every man will respect the dignity and worth of the human personality."
You see, you can kill the dreamer but you cannot kill the dream
It continues to live on in each of us
So we must vow every day to do just one thing to make this world better
And I try every day in my own little corner to leave my fingerprints of goodness on this world
Because I'm her Aunt Nana
She's Cleanna
She's a girl
A Black girl
And I refuse to let life rob her of the belief
That she can leap tall buildings in a single bound.

CHANGE DWELLS IN THE REALM OF THE UNCOMFORTABLE

Martin Luther King once said, "We are now faced with the fact that tomorrow is today. We are confronted with the fierce urgency of now. In this unfolding conundrum of life and history, there "is" such a thing as being too late. This is no time for apathy or complacency. This is a time for vigorous and positive action."
How much more do you need to see?
How much more do you need to hear?
How many articles do you need to read?
How many more discussions will it take?
Our backs are bent from carrying promises of later.
If not now, then when?
When will you set aside the need to feel comfortable. Justice isn't always pretty.
But you don't want to talk about race because it makes you uncomfortable.
You don't want to talk about sexism and misogyny, because it makes you uncomfortable.
You don't want to speak about the sins of history because it doesn't make you feel good.

Let me be crystal clear I am not today, tomorrow, or ever going to change my message so that you can feel good. I am not going to whitewash my message so that it is easier for you to hear. I am not going to water down my message so that you can sleep better at night. I am not going to put blinders on when I speak and pretend that history did not affect why we are where we are today. I refuse to remain silent so that you can rest in comfort, cognitive dissonance.

I am not going to sugarcoat my message, so that is easier for you to swallow. Some medicine simply does not taste good going down. My job is to hold up a mirror to America so that America can catch of glimpse of itself in the past, the present and show a predictive future of where we are heading if we do not make some serious changes. History indeed does repeat itself, and in this slogan to Make America Great Again, some in America are merely trying to rewind time.
It is time for you to get comfortable with being uncomfortable.
I challenge you to understand what being uncomfortable feels like. Burying your 7-year-old granddaughter shot in the head by police while she slept on a couch is uncomfortable.

Having an officer toss you across a classroom like a ragdoll is uncomfortable.
Seeing your son dead in the street for over 4 hours is uncomfortable.
Wondering if your sexuality will be a cause for your death is uncomfortable.
Going to work knowing your boss is going to sexually harass you and don't have the financial luxury to say Me Too is uncomfortable.

Having a police officer wrestle you to the ground in an illegal chokehold while you whisper, "I can't breathe" until you die is uncomfortable. Being told your fiancé has been shot and killed by the police the morning of your wedding is uncomfortable.

Your son going out for Skittles and tea and never coming home again is uncomfortable.
Being raped and the justice system does nothing because you are a Black woman is uncomfortable.

Walking miles to work because you are fighting for the right to sit up front on a bus is uncomfortable.

Getting a phone call that your daughter who was on her way to a new journey in her life is dead on a jailhouse floor is uncomfortable.

Debating if you should wear your hijab and risk being physically assaulted is uncomfortable.
Being told that your son was murdered in jail because the was placed in a shower with water as hot as 180 degrees, is uncomfortable.

Being nervous every single time you get in your car to drive because you are Black is uncomfortable.

Existing in a world where your skin is your sentence, is uncomfortable.

Marginalized people dwell in the realm of uncomfortable every single day.

So now is the time to set aside your dislike of discomfort and move towards action. As Martin Luther King said, "Procrastination is still the thief of time. Life often leaves us standing bare, naked and dejected with a lost opportunity. The "tide in the affairs of men" does not remain at the flood; it ebbs. We may cry out desperately for time to pause in her passage, but time is deaf to every plea and rushes on. Over the bleached bones and jumbled residue of numerous civilizations are written the pathetic words: "Too late." There is an invisible book of life that faithfully records our vigilance or our neglect. "The moving finger writes, and having writ moves on..." We still have a choice today;

Now let us begin. Now let us rededicate ourselves to the long and bitter -- but beautiful -- struggle for a new world. This is the calling of the sons of God, and our brothers wait eagerly for our response. Shall we say the odds are too great? Shall we tell them the struggle is too hard? Will our message be that the forces of

American life militate against their arrival as full men, and we send our deepest regrets? Or will there be another message, of longing, of hope, of solidarity with their yearnings, of commitment to their cause, whatever the cost? The choice is ours, and though we might prefer it otherwise we must choose in this crucial moment of human history."

COMPASSION RISING

On a New York street, a man screams, "I Can't Breathe", as he exhales his final breath
In a Florida nightclub, a man clutches the hand of his lover as he pretends to be dead in a mass shooting
In a South Carolina church 9 men and women are murdered because of the color of their skin
In a Louisville home, a father has buried his 20-year-old daughter killed by senseless violence
In a town in Syria a man buries his twins killed by chemical warfare
Their problems have now become prayers falling on deaf ears
As we continue to exist underneath the veil of compassion
Wearing masks of mirages
Cloaked in the emperor's garments of concern

As Thomas Merton so eloquently penned, "We are living in the greatest revolution in history – a huge spontaneous upheaval of the entire human race: not the revolution planned and carried out by any particular party, race, or nation, but a deep elemental boiling over of all the inner contradictions that have ever been in man, a revelation of the chaotic forces inside everybody. This is not something we have chosen; nor is it something we are free to avoid. This revolution is a profound spiritual crisis of the whole world, manifested largely in desperation, cynicism, violence, conflict, self-contradiction, ambivalence, fear and hope, doubt and belief, creation and destructiveness, progress and regression, obsessive attachments to images, idols, slogans, programs that only dull the general anguish for a moment until it bursts out everywhere in a still more acute and terrifying form. We do not know if we are building a fabulously wonderful world or destroying all that we have ever had, all that we have achieved! All the inner force of man is boiling and bursting out, the good together with the evil, the good poisoned by evil and fighting it, the evil pretending to be good and revealing itself in the most dreadful crimes, justified and rationalized by the purest and most innocent intentions. Man is all ready to become a god, and instead he appears at time to be a zombie."

You see now is not the time for us to slip into slumber
Lying in a bed of illusion
Resting our heads on pillows fluffed with our own concerns
We are no longer able to cover ourselves underneath the blanket of ignorance
Consider this poem the alarm
Now is the time for you to wake up
You have been asleep for far too long

And while you slept
The world has changed
While you slept
Black men and women have been gunned down in the street
While you slept
Women's reproductive rights are being stripped away daily
While you slept
Citizens are fighting for the right to have basic healthcare
While you slept
Wars are being waged daily
While you slept
62 of the richest people in the world have as much wealth as half the world

Houston…we have a problem
You see, I am not writing to entertain you
I am on assignment to shake a nation from its slumber.
And now is the time for you to wake up

You no longer have the choice or luxury to remain silent

Good people were silent during slavery
Good people were silent during the Holocaust
They remained silent when people fought for Civil Rights
They remained silent during the Flint Water Crisis
Good people remained silent during the fight for equality for all people no matter who they loved
Good people remained silent as Black bodies lay in the street
They remained silent when children were bombed in Aleppo
They remained silent as children's bodies washed up on shores
They remained silent as dogs bit those fighting to protect water in Standing Rock
As Burke said, "The only thing necessary for the triumph of evil is for good men to do nothing."

If we are truly going to battle injustice
It will never be accomplished underneath the veil of silence.
We must have the courage to break through the silence and say, "Enough! I stand with them because this is not right!"
Change happens when ORDINARY people stand up and become EXTRAORDINARY.
Oftentimes at the expense of themselves for the uplifting of someone else
You no longer have the right to be a muted bystander
What are you willing to sacrifice?

Can you use your privilege for purpose?
Can you vow not to be muted?
You are chosen for such a time as this
Like Merton said, "You are walking around shining like the sun."
So, shine!
It does not matter what you do. What matters is that you DO SOMETHING!
It is time out for selective vision, pretending that you cannot see the horror, injustice and suffering all around you.
The plane is on fire!
And if we burn, YOU burn too!
There is no way out because as Dr. King said, "We are caught in an inescapable network of mutuality, tied in a single garment of destiny. Whatever affects one directly, affects all indirectly."

My answer to those that ask me, "What can I do?" It is simple. DO YOUR PART! Compassion is found in the small things. Compassion is found in everything. All we must do is look at the humanity in others to see it.

It is the incessant drop of water that can break through a mountain, that can change the world. The revolution is as close as your own front door. Vow to impact those around you. Vow to make a difference in YOUR corner of the world. And be amazed how WE can change the world one act compassion at a time!

SACRED WISDOM OF LOVE

We don't trust love enough
We would rather reject love and embrace fear and hate
instead of allowing our hearts to be open to the possibility that love has the
capability to open the door to true transformation
We don't trust love enough
Trusting means to let your guard down, to strip away your false securities,
judgments, prejudices and reveal your insecurities
Trusting is opening your life to someone that possesses the ability to hurt you in
your frailty
We don't trust love enough
We are too afraid, too settled in our familiar, our comfort, and our convenient
space to step outside of the known and dip our souls into the unknown. We are
scared of getting to know others that do not look like us, that do not think like
us, that challenge our long-held beliefs, our systems and our policies
We are fearful of embracing our differences
Failing to understand that our differences are cause for celebration, for mutual
respect,
understanding and growth
How different our lives, relationships, communities, even this world would be if
just once we decided to trust love
Trust that out of faith, hope and love the greatest of these is love; Trust that it is
okay to love
That love truly can cover a multitude of sins; That loving despite hate is daring
That loving in the face of violence takes courage; That loving in spite of
injustice takes strength
That loving in the face of hurt takes humility
That loving those that society tells you to hate is liberating
Love is a choice. Love is not always a life of convenience. It is an action word.
Loving is not sideline
living. It requires you getting in this game that we call life.
Love takes work especially when it's easy to sit down and say that's not my
problem, why should I care, why should their lives matter? As Thomas Merton
said, "Our job is to love others without stopping to inquire whether or not they
are worthy. That is not our business and, in fact, it is nobody's business. What
we are asked to do is to love, and this love itself will render both ourselves and
our neighbors worthy."
Love is not weakness
Love is still right even when you feel wronged
Love is freedom; It is that quiet resilience in the face of opposition
Love, as Paul gracefully penned, provides us with timeless sacred wisdom

If I speak with human eloquence and angelic ecstasy but don't love, I'm nothing
but the creaking of a rusty gate.

If I speak God's Word with power, revealing all his mysteries and making
everything plain as day,

and if I have faith that says to a mountain, "Jump," and it jumps, but I don't
love, I'm nothing.

If I give everything I own to the poor and even go to the stake to be burned as a
martyr,

but I don't love, I've gotten nowhere.

So, no matter what I say, what I believe, and what I do, I'm bankrupt without
love.

Love never gives up. Love cares more for others than for self.

Love doesn't want what it doesn't have.

Love doesn't strut, doesn't have a swelled head, doesn't force itself on others,

Isn't always "me first,"; Doesn't fly off the handle; Doesn't keep score of the
sins of others,

Doesn't revel when others grovel, Takes pleasure in the flowering of truth,

Puts up with anything, Trusts God always, Always looks for the best,

Never looks back, but keeps going to the end.

Inspired speech will be over some day; praying in tongues will
end; understanding will reach its limit.

But love despite all of the finite things in this world is infinite

Therefore, trust steadily in God, hope unswervingly, love extravagantly.

And the best of all three of these, is love.

Lemonade

Lemonade

Ingredients:

- 4 lbs lemons
- 2 cups water
- 2 cups sugar

Instructions

1. Cut lemons in half.

2. Juice each lemon

3. Keep juicing until you have 2 cups of lemon juice.

4. Pour water into a medium-size saucepan over medium-high heat. Stir in sugar.

5. Continue cooking over heat until sugar is dissolved and liquid looks clear again.

6. Combine sugar solution with lemon juice.

7. When ready to serve, add water to taste.

My Life Lemonade

INGREDIENTS

- PAIN
- LOVE
- HEARTBREAK
- TRAUMA
- JOY
- HAPPINESS
- FAITH
- FRIENDSHIP
- AMAZING SEX
- HUMILITY
- MISTAKES
- PRAYER
- FAILURE
- SUCCESS
- BLACKNESS
- LOVE
- FORGIVENESS

INSTRUCTIONS

MIX IT ALL TOGETHER AND MAKE LIFE AND LOVE OUT OF YOUR MISTAKES AND FAILURES. DON'T WASTE ANYTHING. USE IT ALL THE BITTERNESS AND THE SWEET AND THEN ENJOY THE WAY WALKING IN YOUR PURPOSE AND YOUR DESTINY TASTES.

FINDING ME

If I close my eyes I can see them
If I quiet my myself, I can hear them
Their voices carry on the wind like the tune from chimes floating
in a distant breeze?
Who are you?
Where do you come from?
What is your story?
What languages did you speak?
When you dreamed, what did you dream?
What is your story?
What was your name before they gave you that name?
Was this name passed down through our family?
Am I your descendent?
I stare at my face and wonder if I look like you?
I try to put faces on shadows
Can I find pieces of your memory in cotton fields and red mud?
Can I find you among scattered bones in unmarked graves that
attempt to erase you from history?
You are not (un)Known
You were here
You existed
Because I am here
Through you I exist
I found your name
I found you
And in finding you, I found me…

Amelia County, Virginia. During his lifetime Benjamin Hendrick was "seized & possess'd of a considerable real & personal Estate." In 1777, he bequeathed to his son Barnard "one negro woman named **Hannah** & her Increase & his Plantation & House & 300 acres of Land."

Bill of Sale: Timothy Barham to John Norman, woman by the name of **Hannah** aged 26(?) years and her child named Delia Ann aged one year. $875, 11/25/1852,

North Carolina May 20, 1781
An Inventory (of the Slaves) of the
Estate of JAMES ISBELL, deceased.
Justly and truly given One Negro
woman named *HANNAH* about 26

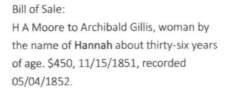

Bill of Sale:
H A Moore to Archibald Gillis, woman by
the name of **Hannah** about thirty-six years
of age. $450, 11/15/1851, recorded
05/04/1852.

POWER

Power
The capacity or ability to influence the behavior of others or the course of
events
Power
Physical might
Power
The energy or motive force by which a physical system or machine is operated
Power
That thing that is placed inside of you
Rumbling deep in your gut
Flowing in your veins
Making your heart beat
That feminine instinct
That allows an ordinary woman to do extraordinary things
That allows a high school drop out to go back to school
That allows a woman beat down to leave an abusive relationship
That gives a woman the strength to say, "I love you but I love myself a little bit
more."
That thing that says not tomorrow
Not when I retire
Not when I turn 40
Not at the start of the New Year
But TODAY
Today is the day
That I will muster up the power within in me to take back everything that was
stolen from me
To fulfill my dreams
To walk away from a job that doesn't pay me what I am worth
To look cancer in the face and say give me your best shot
Today is the day
That I declare diabetes doesn't have to be generational
That the curse of molestation ceases with me
To stop living paycheck to paycheck
That I become a role model to my children
That I recognize if I'm good enough to sleep with than I am good enough to
marry
Today is the day
That the pity party comes to an end
That the time for excuses is over
Today is the day that I declare

I will no longer live defeated
I will not dim my light in order for you to feel brighter
Baby, I was born to shine
I am more than a conqueror
I can do all things through Christ that strengthens me
I am a righteous woman that falls down seven times but gets up eight
I am fearfully and wonderfully made
I am a woman
With unlimited possibilities and infinite potential
I possess the power
To make daydreams reality
To make my life one that matters
Today is the day
That I walk into my destiny
I can be whatever I desire to be
I am whoever I say I am
And today...today I say I am
Strong, Beautiful, Wise, Determined, Intelligent
Gorgeous, Revolutionary, Authentic, Destined for Greatness
I am a woman that loves hard and strong
I am a woman that loves pink frilly things
I am a woman that struts in her stilettos and embraces her curves
unapologetically
I am a woman that loves being a woman
Being treated like a lady
But never attempt to paint me in a corner
Because baby was NEVER meant to be in a corner
My life cannot be defined by coloring in lines
I am 3 hundred and 60 degrees of pure femininity
Bolstered by His promises to me
And today is the day that we access our power
And by doing that
We give permission for another woman to grasp hers
To shine, to grow, to illuminate all that God has placed inside of her
Someone right now, right this very moment, is waiting on you to be all that you
can be
So that they can be all they are destined to be
We are the key to someone's lock
We are the epitome of power
We are strength personified
And together we have the power to change communities, to change policies, to
change lives,
And to finally exhale

Deeply…and just breathe… with ease
Today is the day
We possess our power!

I, Too, Am Serena.
Tales of Being a Black Woman With a Voice

It was the beginning of a New Year, January 2015, the time when everyone starts their, "New Me. New Year," pledges only to find near the end of January they have foregone their resolutions and gone back to everything they vowed they were not going to do. For me, this time it was going to be different. This year I was going to do something different. I was going to take a gamble on me after 16 years of working at a church where I served as the church secretary and the Administrative Assistant to the Pastor. I had been working and writing poetry over the course of 10 years, and it was finally time to make a decision; Hannah do you want to work in this office for the rest of your life or do you want to at least try to do what you know you were destined to do? After 16 years, I was ready to walk into my destiny.

I can recall driving to work each day, sitting in traffic during my 20-minute commute thinking, "There has to be more to life than this. Surely God did not put me on this earth to answer phones, schedule appointments and make copies." Please don't misunderstand me, there is nothing wrong with those things, but I knew in my heart that God was calling me to do something else, something more. I appreciated everything that I learned in my position at the church, but I knew that I was supposed to be writing. There was more that God required of me and I was ready to accept what I was called to do.

I remember I had a conversation with my Pastor at the beginning of the year and I said, "I am leaving this year." I didn't know when and I didn't know how but I knew that 2015 was my year to depart. You know when it is your time to leave, and I knew that I was long overdue. I had grown comfortable in my position, my paycheck, office, parking space and a designated seat on the second pew. But being comfortable is the first stumbling block to change. Being comfortable allows you to linger long after your time has come and gone. And my time at the church was over. At this point, to be honest, I was merely going through the motions. I had done the job so long, I could do it with my eyes closed and make no mistake, I could and did do it well. I took pride in my job and made sure to complete all my tasks with excellence.

But I knew the clock was ticking…

Then, I got a call from a friend to write a poem about power for an event that she was having. She told me that I could write it any way that I wanted as long as the theme was about power and uplifting women. That night I took pen to paper, and I penned my poem entitled, *Power*. In the poem, I wrote several lines that I knew were directed at me because often when poets write they are not writing just to encourage the audience but writing to heal themselves. The day came for me to perform the poem and I will never forget my friend stood at the microphone and said, "Introducing one the greatest writers I have ever known…Hannah Drake," and I started reciting *Power* as I walked through a crowd of one hundred or more women. And then I got to the line, "To have the courage to leave a job that doesn't pay you what you are worth." And I kept reciting, "I will not dim my light in order for you to feel brighter, baby I was born to shine!" And finally, "Today is the day that I step into my destiny!" While the women were on their feet cheering, every line was like a gut punch to my soul! My soul was screaming, "Hannah look into the mirror! You are speaking to yourself!" And I took a long hard look, and I was afraid. Afraid to step out, fearful of the unknown, afraid of what I couldn't see, fearful of failing, afraid of trying. So, after I came down from the high of doing what I was called to do, I rested in my familiarity of being comfortable. But something had shifted. My office felt a little bit smaller, my parking space didn't mean that much to me, my position on the second pew was irrelevant. What was important was that I live, that I fulfill my purpose, that I do what I was destined and designed to do.

My former office

I knew that it was time to go. But each day I continued on the hamster wheel refusing to accept the inevitable.

But God has a way of moving you even when you refuse to budge.

I will never forget the day. It was a Wednesday in November. The leaves had started to die on the trees, winter was settling in. It was time to embrace a new season. Who knew a new season was about to enter my life. I remember sitting in the hallway telling the janitor about setting up a room for a meeting. He refused. To be honest, to this day I cannot remember why he refused, but in hindsight, I can say I now understand his frustrations. However, I was adamant that this room needed to be set up for a meeting, not for me, but for the Pastor and as his assistant that was my utmost duty, to make sure everything that he needed or even thought he needed has already done. The janitor's refusal would leave my job incomplete and as someone that prided herself on the excellence of her work, that was unacceptable. And the janitor and I had words, lots of them. From the hallway all the way down to another office. I do not write this like I am innocent. He was serving up words, and I was serving them right back. No curse words or anything like that but we were both competent in our ability to give a dignified read to one another, and we did.

And then it happened. Out of nowhere this janitor took the papers and manila envelope he had in his hand and hit me in my face. PAUSE! It reminded me of one of those BET movies, record scratch, "I bet you are wondering how I got here…" Did this man just hit me in my face? Then I said, "You bet not do that again!" AND HE DID!! Again, he hit me in my face with the envelopes! I called on God, Jesus, Joseph & Mary not to hit him back. I am from the old school. You hit me, and I hit you back!! But I knew I was in church, and I was the Administrative Assistant to the Pastor, so I was going to have to swallow down this man hitting me not once, but twice! AND I WAS LIVID!!! All the times I had a man put his hands on me flashed in my mind. From my childhood to relationships to now. The very fact that I was in Louisville was behind me and a man fighting. The ONLY reason I came to Louisville was because I was in a battered women's shelter and my father called the shelter, and I happened to pick up the payphone, and he said, "Come home." So I did. My life had been affected and altered by violence, and once I came to Kentucky, I made a vow never to let a man hit me again. And yet here I was in the church with a man hitting me. I told the church secretary what happened and she was floored. She tried to comfort me and calm me down, but that train had already left the station. I went into my office and fought back the tears as I loudly remarked, "You hit the wrong person!" Now that I think about it, "Who would be the right person?" I cannot recall who I called but I knew this information would spread through the church like wildfire and it did. I was angry, I was hurt, I was ashamed, and I was embarrassed. How could this happen to me? I managed to work for almost 20 years with not so much as a complaint and now this.

Silence is lethal...

I went home that night and never said a word. I don't know why. Even today I wish I knew. I slept in a bed of despair blanketed in my anger and shame. Who could I tell this story to? Who would believe me? Even when I thought about it, it seemed crazy and unbelievable to me. How could I leave a life of abuse only to enter a place that should be a sanctuary where I was hit once again? I couldn't wrap my mind around it. And time passed...days...until Monday came and the Pastor walked into my office, and I knew why he was there. He sat across from my desk, and admittedly I felt surely he has my back on this incident. This will just be routine questions that I could and would more than willingly answer. But then the questions shifted as I was asked repeatedly, "Did I hit the janitor?" I never laid a finger on the janitor, and I am the type of person, if I did, I WOULD TELL YOU! I have no reason to lie. It appeared to me that this was going to be the narrative painted, so I sat back in my chair as he continued saying something along the lines of, "The janitor has been let go, and we are going to suspend you for 3 days."
"For what?" I asked.
"For yelling and you could have diffused the situation by not following the janitor down the hall and continuing the conversation."
So, let me get this straight. After 16 years of impeccable service, I am being suspended for 3 days for raising my voice along with another co-worker that was yelling at me? Suspended for having a heated conversation as we BOTH walked down the hall to another office? I tried not to think about all the times I heard other people in the church raise their voices and just focus on the situation at hand. "And then this man hits me not once, but twice, and I am supposed to what, be silent about it?" Interesting. He slides a paper across my desk about my suspension to accept the 3-day suspension and honestly I cannot recall if I signed it or not. I remember I asked, "Can my suspension start now?" He said yes, and I gathered my purse and walked out the door.

A still small voice.

As I was heading home I will NEVER forget, I made it 4 blocks, and as sure as I know my name is Hannah, God said, *"Go back and get your stuff."*
I knew that was it.
That was the door for me to walk into my destiny and I wasn't going to let it close. For one of the FIRST times in my life, I didn't question God, I didn't second guess, I didn't pause. I whipped my car around and headed back to the

church and started packing up my office. It is funny, after 16 years, everything I had of value to me fit in one box. I put that box in my car and headed home, hitting the highway feeling relieved. It was one of the first times that I had stood up for myself. I was not born to go along just to get along. I remember I was at the stoplight at Taylorsville Road and Park Laureate Drive and I called the Pastor and said, "I am done. I don't want to do this anymore. I quit." And for the first time in years, I felt free. Did I have a job lined up? NOPE! Did I have health insurance waiting on me? NOPE! Did I have an endless bank account with money flowing? NOPE! But I had God, me, a pen, and a notepad. I had the me I always wanted to be, free to write and say anything that I wanted to say and that was worth more than all the riches in the world. I started working at the church in my early 20's, and now at almost 40, I was finally able just to be!

So, everything is perfect now, right?

Wrong. After the euphoria of quitting my job wore off, reality set in. I had a daughter in college. I had rent to pay, lights and gas to keep on and food that was needed on the table. But make no mistake when God opens the door, God paves a way. I had a friend that I met with and told what happened, and he said, "How much money would you have made for the remainder of the year?" And I told him, and with no hesitation, he wrote a check for that amount and said, "Now go do what you said you wanted to do. You want to write? Go do that." It all sounds so fairytale happily ever after perfect, but I was hurt. I cried, I yelled, I cried some more. How was this fair? How was this right? I get an email from the Pastor accepting my resignation. It was 3 sentences. After 16 years, it was all summed up in 3 sentences. Then I get an email from the finance department they would finish paying out my salary for the remainder of the year along with my health benefits. Fine. I only asked for one thing when I left, my phone. I had the phone for over 5 years, and I wanted to keep the number and transfer the phone in my name. So I did.

The next few weeks were a haze. How do you find your footing after something so traumatic? After 16 years everything that I knew had shifted. And then my friend came to my house, and she allowed me to cry, and out of the blue she said, "I want you to recite your poem Power." What? How was this the time for a poetry reading? I was having my own personal pity party, how dare she! "I want you to recite your poem, Power," she said again. And so I did. "Power...."
Pause... "Repeat that line again."
"To have the power to leave a job that doesn't pay you what you are worth."
"Say it again."
Tears were streaming down my face, my voice was quivering, but I said, "To have the power to leave a job that doesn't pay you what you are worth."
"Okay keep going."
My voice trembled. "I will not dim my light in order for you to feel brighter, baby

I was born to shine."

"Say it again."

"I will not dim my light in order for you to feel brighter, baby I was born to shine."

She sat with me and made me recite that poem over and over again until I believed it. It wasn't enough for me to stand up in front of other women and recite it, I had to believe it in the core of my being, and finally, I did.

Or so I thought I did.

Still I did not learn.

I remember I applied for a job to be an administrative assistant. Another hamster wheel. Another 9-5 that didn't move me any closer to where I knew I was destined to be. I got the job, and my daughter said, "Mom you JUST left a job doing the same thing. If you really believe that writing is what you are supposed to do, why don't you just try?" *Out of the mouth of babes.* She was right. My fear was keeping me bound. And out of the blue, I had a meeting with two friends, and they offered me a position where I could use my poetry and creativity. Instantly, I knew that was the job for me. I called the other job and told them that I was sorry, but I had to decline the position. It was just a month later, one of the women that hired me for the administrative assistant position heard me speak at an event and came to the stage and told me, "You made the right choice."

I was finally in my zone. I possessed the power to make my daydreams reality. My future, my life wasn't in the hands of anyone else. My destiny had already been written before time was time. God knew the plan before I did and only needed me to align with God's divine will for my life and because God loves us so much, God is willing to shift us BY ANY MEANS NECESSARY! God doesn't dwell in the realm of comfortable! If you are called to do God's will, expect and anticipate the shift! I didn't know what God was doing, but still, I believed. I knew that what God was up to was greater than I could ever imagine.

Forgetting the former things...

Jabez cried out to the God of Israel, "Oh, that you would bless me and enlarge my territory! Let your hand be with me, and keep me from harm so that I will be free from pain." And God granted his request.

1 Chronicles 4:10

By December of 2015, I accepted the new job that would allow me to use my poetry, writing, and creativity in ways that I could never imagine. I entered into January 2016, and my friend gifted me with the Prayer of Jabez book, and I said, "I am just going to start praying this prayer and see if it is true." And in weeks after writing poetry for almost 20 years, my poem Formation went viral and literally went around the world. My new job has taken me across the United States, using poetry to elevate and amplify the voices of those this world often forgets. I have been to Mississippi, Philadelphia, New York, Alabama, Washington DC, New Orleans, North Carolina just to name a few places. While this may not seem like a lot to some people, this is coming from a woman that never traveled. At 39 years old, I finally got my passport and poetry allowed to travel to Dakar, Senegal. Poetry allowed me to step foot in the Motherland. What is even more exciting for me, is my liberation allowed my daughter to get her passport and she made the trip to Dakar with me. That is how freedom works. It is not just for ourselves, but our freedom allows other people to live free. When I told my daughter that I was going to write this blog, she said, "Mom I am proud of you." In January 2017, I started my blog, and my very first blog went viral. From there people read my blog all around the globe. I have been invited to write for Cosmopolitan, my blog entitled Do Not Move Off The Sidewalk ignited a movement that landed me on Inside Her Story with Jacque Reid and Tom Joyner, my poem Spaces was selected by the National Academy of Medicine as one of the 30 pieces of artwork that speak to visualizing health equity, I was selected as one of the first Hadley Creatives in Louisville, and I was nominated to be the first Black female Poet Laureate of Kentucky.

I remember when I returned to church for a meeting and I went into my old office and I was stunned by how small everything looked and my friend said, "You are much too big for this office now, Hannah." And I smiled. I had outgrown my position a long time ago. No one has a light and hides it under a bushel and greatness cannot be contained. I remained hidden in that office for far too long but there comes a time in life that God will no longer allow you to be hidden.

God has blown my mind! And I wouldn't take nothing for the journey! Everything that I had to go through to get this point showed me, "Hannah do not be afraid to be a woman with a voice! Do not be afraid to stand up for yourself! Do not be afraid to raise your voice! Do not be afraid to shout when the world demands that you whisper! Do not be afraid to walk in your authority!"

To my women, particularly Black women, I know. I hear you. I see you. I understand that this world will tell you that you are too much. When I watched Serena stand up for herself, my story came flooding back, and I knew I had to share it. Too often Black women are penalized for being loud, and our passion is characterized as anger. We are punished for the bad behavior of some men. We are called ghetto when some of the greatest minds in the world have come out of the bricks. We are considered to be having a meltdown when we stand up for ourselves. We are made into caricatures, depicted as Jim Crow images, wide hipped and big-lipped when we demand respect. Demand it anyways. Stand up anyways. Even if your knees are knocking and your voice is quivering, speak boldly. And when you stand up, know that like Serena and me, it may cost you. You may have to give up one thing, to gain EVERYTHING! But know that the price of your silence will be far more costly.

You have a voice, do not be afraid to use it! If this world tells you that you are too much, they just cannot handle the woman you are designed to be. Be that woman anyways! Just do it! Shout it from the rooftops that you are here, loud, proud, bold and unashamed!

BLACK SWANS SWIMMING UPSTREAM

I am uncertain
If it was
Safety, Sanctuary or Sisterhood
That caused us to instinctively migrate towards one another like elegant black
swans amongst a lake of white lilies
Yet there we found ourselves amongst one another
Able to take off our armor
Speak in our vernacular
Understood one another without needing to say words

It was there in the 'uh huh', 'girrrrrl', 'no she didn't', 'they tried it' and high-
fives
That we spoke in a dialect that conjured up thoughts of cornbread, catfish,
collard greens and cornrows

For a moment, we could just be sister girls

We laughed and sipped wine
Ate food made for small bites not for mouths shaped like ours that spoke loudly
in the key of rage and justice

We knew we would have to leave one another
Disperse ourselves amongst the crowd so we would not be seen as "that
group", "those people" "those Black women" all huddled together

We stood
Strengthened to go back into those spaces amongst the lilies

But for a moment we were just sistas
Finding the power in one another to swim upstream...

FOR COLORED GIRLS WHO CONSIDERED SUICIDE WHEN LEMONADE IS ENUF

This is a poem for colored girls
Hold Up
I said, this is a poem for colored girls who have considered suicide when
Lemonade is Enuf
This is a poem for colored girls who were never told that their skin radiates
drops of sunlight like spotlights, that the coils that spring from their head is
good hair because He created it and He said, "It is good."
This is a poem for colored girls that were told that they were too black, too
light, too fat, too skinny, their lips were too big, their voices too loud, that they
were just too much of everything
This is a poem for every colored girl that has built Sandcastles near watery
shores, for every colored girl that stayed up All Night staring at bedroom doors
praying that for just one night he wouldn't creep in...
For every colored girl whose soul is parched, that loved completely and
recklessly and still found themselves broken and alone in a Love Drought
This is a poem for colored girls that sit in solitude in darkened
rooms…waiting…as the spirits of our ancestors listen, praying to catch us
whispering, "Show me, Guide Me, Share with me" secrets that have yet to told
In our prayers we discover our strength, our courage, our power
Our voice
No longer will we say Sorry
No longer will we apologize for simply existing
Don't Hurt Yourself in an attempt to silence a shout
A caged animal will always roar for Freedom
So simply let it be…let us be
Everything that we are destined to be
We were born placing our feet into footprints of greatness
We carry the mantle of women that have gone before us, paving the way
We will no longer water down our existence to make you feel comfortable
This is who we are in all our "colored-ness" and it is glorious
Full strength, pure, raw, undiluted
We make this look easy
Yet we carry the weight of a nation on calloused feet shoved into 6 inch heels
We carry the wisdom of Momma and Daddy Lessons
We learned how to survive by any means necessary
We are mountain movers
Determined to only glance behind us to see where we have been so we know
where we do not want to return
Our mission is simple…to move Forward

Onward, bringing another woman along the journey
Standing together in full Formation
Recognizing that when life gives you lemons
Smile, graciously and make Lemonade
Then pause, take a seat, relax your soul and sip slowly, take it all in
This is for you, for us, for the women that have gone on before us and the
women that will come after us
This is For Colored Girls Who Have Considered Suicide When Lemonade is
Enuf...

BREAK YOURSELF

"Bring them here to me," Jesus said.
Taking the five loaves and the two fish and looking up to heaven,
he gave thanks and broke the loaves.
Then he passed them to the disciples, and the disciples passed them to the
people. Mark 14:18

I dare you to break yourself

I dare you to hand your destiny to God
Ask God to take it
To Break it
And then pass it

There is beauty in the breaking
But you have sold an illusion

The Power is not in pretending
It is not in a living a life that is a lie
The Power is not in the filtered image that you present to the world
The Power is in having the courage to break yourself
To stand up and speak your truth
Even when you are afraid
There is power in sharing your story
There is power in telling another woman how you made it over

I dare you to break yourself
To tell another woman your testimony
Because there are women waiting on you that are hungry for the truth
That need your story to make it to the other side

Tell her how you left a man that did nothing but use your body as punching bag
Tell her how you managed to feed three kids on a single mother's income
Tell her how you woke up one day decided that you were worth it
Tell her how you survived a marriage after the affair
Tell her how you overcame childhood abuse
Tell her how you battled and won when you faced addiction
Tell her how you find your joy and happiness after all hell breaks loose
Tell her there is nothing too hard for God
Tell her what this world meant for evil in her life, God meant it for good

Let her know that God isn't breaking her to destroy her
God is breaking her to build her
God is breaking her to make her
God is breaking her to position her
God is breaking her for a purpose that is bigger than herself
God is breaking her to pass her story to others so that they can be fed

Your breaking is not just for you
It is intertwined with the life of another woman
Your brokenness creates pieces of a puzzle for other women to delivered
Your brokenness allows another woman to be set free
Your brokenness gives another woman the courage to stand in her truth
To show up as her authentic self with no apologies needed

God is asking you to be like the little boy with the 5 loaves of bread and two fish, "Bring it to me!"
Your sickness, bring it to me
Your pain, bring it to me
Your heartache, bring it to me
Your dreams, bring it to me
Your relationship, bring it to me
Bring it all to me and watch me blow your mind!

Imagine the Power of women coming together
Standing together
Praying together
Laughing together
Rejoicing together
Building together
Exhaling together

What is the Power of women breaking themselves?

What is the Power of women knowing their deliverance is in their breaking
Their healing is in their breaking
Their joy is their breaking
Their testimony is in their breaking
Their potential is in their breaking
Their very destiny is in their breaking

So stand
And have the courage
To allow God to take you

Break you
And then pass you
And be amazed by how women standing in their truth can make the ground
tremble and begin change the world!

DAWN

Dawn
The first appearance of light
the beginning,
birth,
inception,
genesis,

An emergence,
An appearance,
An arrival,

to begin,
to start,
to be born,
to appear,
to arrive,
To rise
To break
To unfold,
To develop
To become evident to the mind; be perceived or understood.

Every day that we awake it is a new dawn
A chance to start over
To begin again
To birth something new
To show Patience
To love

To offer forgiveness
To understand
To try
To heal
To lose ourselves to find ourselves
To dream
To dance
To believe
To show compassion
To give

To say, "I'm sorry."
To breathe
To exhale
To take it all in
To dare
To take a chance

What is your dawn?
What is your new day?
What awaits you on the horizon of change?

"Hope begins in the dark, the stubborn hope that if you just show up and try to do the right thing, the dawn will come. You wait and watch and work: you don't give up"*

What could we be if we weren't afraid?
What could we become if we loved?
If we embraced our differences
If we celebrated our uniqueness
If we chose to disregard our fear and love anyway?

Who could we be?
What could we accomplish?
How high could we soar?
Didn't you ever dream of flying?
If you take my hand together we can.
Nothing would be impossible if we stood together.

A new day awaits us
All we have to do is rise and greet the dawn.

*Anne Lamott

I AM BECOMING

To Change
To Adjust
To Transform

To Transition
To Bend
To Break

To Move
To Grow
To Learn

To Become

As the Apostle Paul penned,
"Not that I have already attained, or am already perfected; but I press on, that I
may lay hold of that for which Christ Jesus has also laid hold of me. Brethren, I
do not count myself to have [b]apprehended; but one thing I do, forgetting those
things which are behind and reaching forward to those things which are
ahead, 14 I press toward the goal for the prize of the upward call of God in
Christ Jesus."

I have not yet attained
I have not yet become
But I press towards the mark

I am in the process of becoming

So I embrace my metamorphosis
I will no longer hide
I am no longer ashamed
Acknowledging that everything that I have experienced led me to this moment

This is my truth
My journey
My evolution
To becoming the woman that I am destined to be

There were times that I did not understand
That I wanted this cup to pass from me
That I didn't want to face the pain of my reality
Why me are two words that are real

But I've learned the answer to that question

My pain was a pathway to my purpose

So let me be(come) what I be

You see
I be's
Deformed destinies
Hunchbacked haikus
Dreams deferred

I be's…life
Tattered
Bruised
Enraptured
Beat down
Loved
Stomped on
Abused

So let me be(come)

I be's…Power
A shout in a room filled with whispers
The flow of the Nile
David's psalms
Africa's drumbeat
Eric Garner's last words
I be's Nina Simone's blackbird
Paul Dunbar's mask
Maya's knowledge of why the caged bird sings at last

So let me be(come)

I be's
Nas's one mic

Robert Frost's road not taken
Langston's raisin in the sun
I be Mike Brown's hands
I be's revolution
So let me be (come)
Let me be
Loud
Fearless
Magnificent and Brilliant
Let me be rhythm
Let me be the womb of our ancestors
Let me be restored
Let me marvelous, authentically us.
Let me be Africa's heartbeat
Let us be great, dynamic, breathtaking
Let me be light
Let me love and revolution and lemonade

Let me be…everything.

I AM BECOMING!

LOVE, REVOLUTION, & LEMONADE

It's funny, when people hear me speak about my life they think, "No way. There is no way Hannah came from that, to now be this." I just smile.
No one would ever imagine the roads I walked, barefoot, begging and bleeding.

Yet, here I am.

Imperfect in every single way imaginable doing the impossible. I always say, "I am just an ordinary woman that has been blessed to extraordinary things."

When I tell you it can only be because God ordained my footsteps, trust that. I am simply a mercy and grace case. There are so many times I failed. So many times I got on my knees and prayed and bargained with God only to wake up and do the same shit over and over again. You can lie to everyone else, but you cannot lie to the person staring back at you in the mirror. She knows the truth, even as much as you try to hide it.

I don't know why God continues to forgive me. I can only imagine it's because of God's mercy and grace. I don't know why God continues to use me but trust me, if God can use me, God can use anyone. One of my favorite scriptures in the Bible is, Jeremiah 29:11, "For I know the plans I have for you," declares the LORD, "plans to prosper you and not to harm you, plans to give you hope and a future."

My plans must be bigger than my failures.

I wish I could write something profound to make you feel that I was special and unique but I can't.

And I believe that is the beauty of this book.

I am a hodgepodge of glory, and shit, excellence and imperfection. I am a kaleidoscope of shades of anger and rage, of love and happiness, of sadness and depression.

I am beauty and ugly. I am erotic and stand-offish. I am sensual and soft. I am passionate. I pull you close only to push you away. I am greatness intertwined with failure. I am human. I am me.

I am a woman that lives her life in shades of gray but when I speak, I speak in color. My tongue is like a loom and it weaves words of indigo, crimson, bronze, and gold. When I write, I write marvelous shades of magenta and marigold and periwinkle and rose. Everything is bursting in color. I use these words to light my path in the darkness, using the words to illuminate my soul.

I am a woman that is trying, that is striving, that is living...that is becoming.

All I did was take the lemons that life handed me and made lemonade.

So I dare you to make lemonade.

With Love & Revolution,
Hannah Drake

ABOUT THE AUTHOR

Hannah L Drake is a blogger, activist, public speaker, poet, and the author of 9 books. She writes commentary on politics, feminism, and race and her work has been featured in Cosmopolitan Magazine. In 2019 during Super Bowl Sunday, Hannah's poem, "All You Had To Do Was Play The Game, Boy," which addresses the protest by Colin Kaepernick, was shared by film writer, producer and director Ava DuVernay, and then shared by Kaepernick. The poem has been viewed more than two million times.

Hannah was selected by the Muhammad Ali Center to be a Daughter of Greatness which features prominent women engaged in social philanthropy, activism, and pursuits of justice. Hannah has presented at the Idea Festival, curated performances for the Festival of Faiths, partnered with The Louisville Ballet for their Choreographer's Showcase, shared the stage with activist Angela Davis, and exhibited her visual art and poetry at the Kentucky Museum of Art and Craft. Her poem "Spaces" was selected by the National Academy of Medicine as 1 of 30 pieces of art that speak to health equity. Hannah was selected as a 2017 Hadley Creative by the Community Foundation of Louisville and Creative Capital and her work has been honored by the Kentucky Alliance of Against Racist and Political Repression.

Hannah Drake was featured on the Tom Joyner Morning Show with Jacque Reid to discuss her movement, "Do Not Move Off The Sidewalk," which addresses the power of holding your space. Hannah's message is thought-provoking and at times challenging, however, Hannah believes that change dwells in the realm of the uncomfortable. "My sole purpose in writing and speaking is not that I entertain you. I am trying to shake a nation."

Facebook: Hannah Drake
Twitter: HannahDrake628
Instagram: HannahDrake628
www.hannahldrake.com
www.writesomeshit.com

53654104R00077

Made in the
USA
Lexington, KY